Unravelled

by Briony Marshall

Published by TWH Publishing;
Independent Publishing House, West Yorkshire
www.thewritinghall.co.uk

Cover design by Charlie O'Neill;
www.sebandcharliedesign.co.uk

ISBN 978-1-9998669-0-7

Printed in the UK by Grosvenor Group Ltd, Loughton, Essex IG10 3TS

For My Mom

*The first person to teach me how to truly
appreciate a ball of wool*

Chapter One

"Appreciate your beginnings before you start searching for the end"

'Perhaps if you took fewer steroids and more Viagra, we wouldn't have that problem!'

As the words left Claire's lips she knew there was no going back. In the heat of the argument, at the very point of the volcano's eruption, she'd retorted with the only weapon she had.

She spat every syllable, hoping that each one would hit him like the verbal dagger he'd just thrown. She must have succeeded because, for the first time in their two-year relationship, Muscles fell silent.

Muscles, as Claire 'affectionately' called her boyfriend, was the stereotypical testosterone-filled gym bunny, who preached the importance of health and fitness to anyone who'd listen. Tonight's argument had been more than a lovers' tiff or cute quarrel, and it had gone well beyond the realms of those sweet little differences that made opposites attract. It had been a verbal riot.

A war that had ended when Muscles threw out the biggest insult Claire had ever heard in her whole entire life.

Muscles had entered his flat in the same way he did every Thursday evening. He'd thrown his hoodie at the pegs in the hall, strode into the kitchen, removed his vest and tossed it in the laundry bin. 'Hey, honey, what's cooking?' He sniffed the air expectantly.

This was usually Claire's cue to mumble something about beans and toast, or ham, bread and the toastie-maker. But tonight, Claire had been sat at the kitchen table, Muscles' laptop open before her, her eyes staring at the screen with a steely-eyed determination.

Muscles peered over her shoulder. 'Click 'n' Food?' His voice was laced with disgust. *'Takeaway?'*

Claire was making a stand. She was sick of the comments he made every week, about how toasting a slice of bread or boiling an egg 'wasn't technically cooking'; how noodles in a pot of boiling water 'didn't count as a proper meal'; or being told, for the umpteenth time, that, after doing the long shift at work 'that hers wasn't really appropriate food to come home to'.

Claire remembered their seventh date; she'd watched in awe as Muscles created an elaborate pasta dish. As she'd consumed the delicious meal, Claire found herself confessing her culinary shortcomings.

Back then, Muscles had deemed it 'an irrational fear'. 'You just need to grab the bull by the horns, Claire,' he'd said. So, for the last two years, Thursday nights had been reserved for culinary tuition. Muscles guided Claire through the world of cooking, one dish at a time.

But following a promotion and subsequent change of his shifts at the gym, Thursday nights meant Claire had full control of the kitchen. At first it had been fun. A challenge… which sometimes equalled disaster; sometimes, a miracle.

'I'm not eating takeaway! Have you even thought about the carbs in a dish like that? Let alone the sugars and the additives…and the *fat!*' Muscles shouted from the bedroom as he got changed. 'Throw one of your famous potato cake extravaganzas in the toaster, and we'll forget this ever happened. Okay?'

Claire continued to type, her fingers quivering over the keys. Rage began to brew. 'No.'

She heard Muscles scoff. 'Babe, come on, stop messing about. You are what you eat, remember? And I pride myself on not being a takeaway.'

Claire often wondered why she was with a guy like Muscles. Some days she could imagine that, despite their differences, there really was some underlying passionate force pulling them together like magnets. Most days, however, she was aware that their bond was simply down to habit.

She had a history of clinging to things, rather than stretching her independence. And the pattern had only continued: tolerating Muscles' snide remarks and controlling nature because it was easier and less scary than braving life alone. Muscles represented 'playing it safe', as did ordering a takeaway because she was scared of cooking up another disaster. Habits were hard to break, but change was on the horizon.

She got up and stood in the bedroom doorway, her arms crossed over her chest. 'I'm ordering a takeaway.'

Muscles had his back to her. His arms looked like they'd been modelled on King Kong's, and he boasted a six-pack that would rival any off-licence's. His physique was at its peak, which was probably to be expected of a personal trainer, but at that moment Claire did not much care for the Greek God before her.

He wore nothing but a pair of skin-tight black boxers, which exaggerated every millimetre of his pert bottom; all Claire could do was glare at it as it waggled around in front of her. 'Wow, wow, wow...honey, what's all this about?' Muscles narrowed the space between them. 'You and I both know you're better than this,' he said, gently caressing Claire's cheek.

She kept her glare. 'I just don't fancy cooking tonight.'

Muscles rolled his eyes. 'You don't fancy cooking any night, babe. I mean, come on, eggy bread is barely a breakfast, let alone a main meal.'

That's it! Button, pressed. 'Exactly, Peter, which is why I'm letting someone else do the cooking for a change.'

'You only cook on a Thursday night! Any other time, it's either me or your parents slaving over the stove. Pick up some of the slack for a change.'

His bottom wiggled again. Many a time Claire had gazed at that same bottom as she wondered how she'd managed to attract someone as physically gifted as Muscles. His rear seemed a fitting representation of how she saw him that

3

Thursday night: cold, hard, and full of shit.

'Fine, I will.' She turned on her heel and sat back at the laptop.

'You're not even thinking of my needs!' Muscles whined.

'Just lift a few more weights in the morning. One take-away isn't going to hurt.' Claire tapped away at the key-board.

Muscles came into the kitchen and grabbed an apple from the fruit bowl. 'Now you're just being selfish,' he said, taking a noisy bite.

'I'm trying to buy you food. How is that being selfish?' Claire could feel a headache coming on and her patience wearing thin.

'Because I don't want it!' he said, spraying bits of apple everywhere.

'Either eat it, or cook for yourself. I'm bored of trying to please you, Peter.'

The pair fell silent. Muscles appeared to be processing her statement, and Claire didn't want to talk any more. She'd made her decision.

'I'm still not going to eat it.'

'I'm still going to order it.'

Muscles uttered something unintelligible, then snapped, 'Just give me that.' He reached for the laptop.

'No.'

'Give me my laptop!'

'Get off! I'm almost done.'

Both had hold of one side of the laptop; neither showed any sign of letting go. A tug-of-war ensued as Click 'n' Food processed Claire's order.

Suddenly, Muscles let go. 'For God's sake, Claire! Why do you have to be so immature?'

She froze, the laptop clutched to her chest. She couldn't possibly have heard him correctly; she even contemplated asking him to say it again. Then, when realisation hit, she snapped.

'Immature? *Immature?!* Last time I looked, I was an adult with a full-time job, a stable income, and what I believed to be – until ten seconds ago - a serious relationship.'

'An adult? You're not even a fully-fledged human being! You're immature and incapable. Being able to cook something more than beans on toast or a boiled egg is a basic life skill.'

Claire didn't know what to say. Their spat had left the realms of 'to takeaway or not to takeaway'. Plus, Muscles' argument sounded rehearsed.

'And while we're at it, so is a driving licence, for crying out loud! I even had to nudge you to update your bus pass photo not too long ago, because you were still using the one from college. You're twenty-eight, Claire. Me and you, we should be moving on, moving forward, thinking about bigger things…our own place, our own lives, our own family. I've had my flat the whole time I've known you. I've lost count of the number of times I've asked you to move in. But all you want to do is stay at home with your parents. That qualifies as not only bizarre, but a massive turn off!'

He may as well have slapped her. *A family? A house?* All Claire had wanted was a takeaway, not a mirror held up to her life. She was hurt. She wanted her words to burn as much as his. That's when she'd suggested – nay, *screamed* – that he should ease off the steroids in favour of Viagra if a family was part of his plan.

Muscles' breath caught in his throat and there was a long pause. 'That's it. I've had enough. All you do is weigh me down.'

'What? Like one of your stupid dumbbells?'

Muscles brought his hands to his head in exasperation. 'You don't know anything about weights, fitness, or even dietary requirements, for that matter. Don't even try!'

'I do know one takeaway won't kill you. Heaven forbid, you might even enjoy it!'

'Why would you want to turn this,' Muscles gestured down his body: his broad shoulders, washboard abs, tiny waist and muscular thighs, 'into *that?*' He gestured towards Claire, whose stare hardened.

'This isn't about the food anymore,' said Claire.

Muscles gave her a slow clap. 'Bravo! You're finally getting it.'

'So, it's just *my* lack of maturity, is it? Just because I don't drive, or own a fancy car. Maybe I love my body just the way it is. And perhaps I've never wanted to move in with you, into this poxy flat, because I'd become more of a gym widow than I already am!'

'Why are you still hanging around then, if that's how you really feel?' he sneered.

Claire's mind knew why: *stability, comfort, habit.* 'Because I used to believe in compromise.'

Muscles gave a sarcastic laugh. 'You've proven tonight that you don't understand the meaning of the word. I don't know why I ever thought this could work. We have absolutely nothing in common.' He paused, but only for a heartbeat. 'I'm starting to wish I'd never met you.'

This was it.

'Well, that's where you're wrong…we do have something in common. I wish I'd never met you, too!' she screeched.

The doorbell made both of them jump.

'I think you'd better leave.' His lips had clamped into a straight line.

'Gladly.' Claire lifted her coat from the back of the chair, stomped towards the door, then pushed the button marked 'Open'. Muscles turned his head away as she passed.

The delivery guy didn't get chance to say a word before she snatched the food bundle from his arms. 'He'll pay,' she shouted, as she dashed down the stairs.

Claire stood in the wet and cold, the last bus of the evening her only option. As she waited at the stop across from Muscles' flat, she tried to process everything that had happened. She looked up at his kitchen window, a glimmer of hope in her mind that his shadow would appear, see her standing in the rain, and beckon her back inside.

Surely this can be sorted? Arguments are healthy in relationships, right?

It wasn't long before hope turned to reality, which was a twenty-minute wait for the bus, and a soggy Indian banquet under her armpit.

Chapter Two

"If at first you don't succeed, try, try, and just keep trying"

Claire sat at her desk, knitting needles in hand, stitches in place, pattern at the ready, and dishevelled ball of vivid red wool beside her. Knitting, to Claire, was usually a source of peace, but today she was not making the rhythmic click click of a knitter at ease. In fact, the only noise in the room came from the clock, tick-ticking her sanity away.

Even knitting can't turn a doctor's surgery into a place of calm and relaxation. She could sense the patients' fear and anxiety. After the fortnight from hell, Claire's place of work had turned from merely uncomfortable to almost unbearable. She'd turned to her knitting for comfort, believing a new life would start with a new project. But even that wasn't going her way.

'For crying out loud!' she muttered. 'I can't even cast on now.' She jabbed at her stitches, strangulating them with the yarn as it passed through, before shoving them over to her other needle, each movement punctuated with a grunt or tut.

At what age does it become an embarrassment to say you still live with your parents? This was the one thought Claire had been unable to budge for weeks. Her dispute with Muscles was still driving her crazy.

Claire had been happy. Well, maybe not happy. *Content.* She'd managed to be in a relationship with the same guy for over two years. That was an achievement in itself. Her self-proclaimed mediocre relationship, which her friends referred to as 'being practically hitched', had outlasted the record of her best friend, and was double the length of her perfect cousin Flora's fluke of a marriage.

Even Claire's parents had written her off as a lost cause. In their opinion, she was doomed for a marriage way below their expectations.

Blah, blah, blah. Insert Austen novel here.

They thought Claire could do better, but, for her, Muscles had been okay, and okay was all she was after.

She'd understood that they weren't exactly compatible; his gym addiction and her passion for all things woolly didn't mix well. In fact, Claire's idea of exercise was her daily battle with her unruly red hair.

Muscles' hobbies included blowing his money on over-priced protein shakes and passing comment on strangers' body types (which often included a not-so-quiet rundown of the gruelling workout routines they needed to undergo 'to sort themselves out'). In comparison, Claire enjoyed spending many a quiet hour creating fabulously bizarre knitted creations for her nearest and dearest. And, although she was aware they were two very different people, not once had she deemed it a problem. Until now.

They'd spoken only once since the argument: over the phone, to arrange a suitable time for Muscles to collect his dumbbells from her parents' study. His obsession with the gym had even spread to her family home, and if this was it, then those dumbbells were the first things she wanted out of her sight. She would have thrown them into the street just to annoy him, but neither she nor her parents could lift them.

If she'd thought there was a second chance for her and Muscles it was pushed into the land of no return the evening he called to collect his weights. Claire was at work when he came for them, but when taking out the rubbish later that evening, she found the dumbbell cosies she'd lovingly hand-knitted chucked in the dustbin. There was no going back.

Her singleton status commanded a review of her life; once Muscles was out the picture, she realised that her personal and professional achievements equated to zero.

She'd dreamed of achieving things: visiting at least five different countries, learning a language, to pass her driving test, land her dream job…*to find the person she wanted to be with for the rest of her life.*

Yet, she'd got nowhere.

Her parents had always tried to push her further; when she left school, they'd urged her to study for a degree at the prestigious university just out of town. Instead, she'd taken a secretarial diploma at the local training centre.

They'd seen Claire behind a marble desk in a grand office building. Their disappointment, therefore, was clear when Claire gleefully announced that she'd got a job at a doctor's surgery.

'Oh, Claire, that's wonderful!' her mum had said. 'In Harley Street?'

'Erm, no. Doctor Leach's practice. You know, on Dovedon Road?'

Her mother's face could have curdled milk.

That was ten years ago, and Claire *still* worked there. It wasn't as if it was her dream either; what she really wanted was to be a personal assistant to the stars. She longed to see the world whilst taking gratification from the fact someone else needed her. But it was a pipe dream; Claire had become comfortable with her life, and that was the issue.

Now Muscles had gone, were other changes on the horizon?

'Hello, Claire. Are you okay?' Claire snapped back to reality and met the concerned face of Mildred Humphrey, the person behind the local delicacy 'Sprout Surprise'. As a frequent visitor to the surgery, they were on first name terms.

'Sorry, Mildred. I'll check you in right away. Please take a seat.' Claire gestured to the chairs and continued to tap away at her keyboard whilst Mildred shuffled to a seat directly opposite. When Claire looked up from her screen she noticed Mildred watching her with squinty eyes. Claire shifted awkwardly in her seat.

Unnerved by Mildred's constant eye contact, Claire looked down at her knitting. She sighed. She couldn't understand it. Four measly rows, and her tension was off; the stitches were uneven, and, instead of the work being a straight piece, it was already veering off to the left. It looked clumsy and out of sync, nowhere near the standard she usually achieved.

Claire had always loved the craft, ever since her grandma had taught her to knit tiny woollen jumpers and cardigans for her dolls. It was a talent that had grown with her, but ever since the argument with Muscles any attempt at knitting had turned out a disaster.

She attempted to save this latest project, to prove that it was just a coincidence. But, as her hands fumbled over the stitches, they remained as sloppy and disorganised as ever. 'Story of my life,' she muttered, clutching the woollen wreckage.

She was relieved to find that Mildred had shuffled off to the waiting room toilets. As she gazed across the rest of the room, her hopelessness was magnified. Claire had nicknamed Wednesday afternoons 'the OAP party'. The patients crowding the surgery were the same crestfallen faces she saw every week, each one utterly convinced they were on death's door - that, if they didn't inform the doctor, weekly, of every ache, pain, sniffle, cough, body change, mole or wrinkle, they wouldn't survive the night.

They didn't just bring their problems, they also brought trouble. Mr Jackson, for instance, had come to complain about his medication. Again. At least this time he hadn't insisted that his blood pressure medication was fitted with a tiny tracker device and microphone. That had been a fun hour - insisting that she didn't work for the FBI, that Doctor Leach was not an undercover spy, and that no one in the surgery believed Mr Jackson was an alien.

Then there was Mr and Mrs Baxter, at the surgery for their flu jabs, and about to celebrate their golden wedding anniversary. They'd spent those fifty years in 'wild, exotic love' and weren't ashamed to share the details. Claire knew perfectly well, when Mrs Baxter had asked for the number of the GUM clinic, that she hadn't meant the dentist.

Last was Mrs Spencer, collecting the results of her blood tests. She'd once managed to lock herself in the waiting room toilet - the only problem was, she hadn't checked in with Claire first. It wasn't until Mrs Parker had almost wet herself (after waiting more than half-an-hour to use the facilities) that Claire had been forced to investigate. The fire brigade eventually discovered that Mrs Spencer had fallen asleep on the loo.

Claire wondered if she should focus on her own health - perhaps offload the responsibility of making herself better onto someone else. Maybe then she'd feel happier. But all Claire had on her list of ailments were a few war wounds to her self-esteem. Plus, if anyone else was to prove the source of her cure, it wouldn't be Dr Leach.

The shrill ring of the telephone broke through the grunts and splutters. Claire jumped at the sound, and felt her knitting needle fall from her grip and out of its stitches. It hit the floor, its hollow metal making a tinny sound. Her teeth clenched. She didn't dare look at the catastrophe across her knees, and instead, reached for the receiver.

'Good afternoon, Dovedon Surgery. How may I help you? Hello. Yes, Mrs Willabee. No, not yet. Urine samples usually take at least a week. Yes, I know. We'll ring if there's an emergency. Yes, yes. Okay. Okay, thank you, Mrs Willabee. Bye, bye.' It was the third time Mrs Willabee had called that week.

I know the poor lady is worried, but that is taking the p-

Claire shook the thought loose. Her low mood wasn't an excuse to take the mickey out of the patients. She took a deep breath and checked the time.

3.32pm. Only an hour until home time.

'Next patient, please,' Doctor Leach's voice crackled over the intercom. Claire went to call Mrs Cotton through when a smell best described as yesterday's 'Sprout Surprise' poisoned her nostrils. The stench was so overwhelming it took Claire a moment to gather her thoughts. Mildred returned to her seat, a satisfied smirk on her face. Claire bit her tongue. Being gassed by a patient was just another irritant to add to her list. She chanced a quick breath. *Rise above it. You're a professional.*

She smiled sweetly at the bodies in the waiting room and adopted the false high-pitched receptionist voice she'd developed so well over the years. 'Mrs Cotton? Please go through.'

Claire ignored murmured complaints about the smell wafting around the waiting room and bent down for her rebellious needle. She assessed the damage; the point was, luckily, still intact. However, the five rows she'd spent the afternoon creating were pitiful. If she continued, the only person who'd ever wear the jumper would be the scarecrow on her father's allotment.

The effort needed to recapture all the tiny loops on one pin seemed too much at that moment. *Too painful, too intense.*

Instead, she set about unravelling her work and prepared for the fifth cast on row of the day. She sighed and placed the fragments of her knitting in her lap, then reached for the can of air freshener stashed under the desk.

Is this living?

Chapter Three

"Self-discipline is key; know when enough is enough"

In the weeks that followed Claire didn't exactly help herself. Grown women, when confronted with the idea that their self-worth is a big fat zero, and they're stranded on Single-ton Island, often experience a sudden rush of independence.

'Nothing or no one can stand in my way!' they chant.

But Claire had gone in the other direction. She went from being a feisty young woman to broken-hearted teen in the blink of an eye.

The decor of her room normally boasted a sophisticated vintage look, but now it was swamped with empty food packets and fizzy drink bottles. A congealed box of cheese from last Saturday's pizza feast had taken up residence under her bed, alongside the sticky remains of a spilt energy drink. Her bedside table, normally clear and tidy, was practically invisible under layers of receipts, takeaway menus, wrappers and coffee rings.

As for her appearance: her hair, unruly though socially acceptable, was a frizzy mass. It stuck out at odd angles - to even hope for a good hair day, Claire had to slather on extreme hold gel and extra strength hairspray to keep it tamed.

Claire's make-up was minimalist by rule anyway, but right now it was non-existent. It felt like a chore and too much effort; regardless of the amount of concealer she used, her under-eye circles were getting darker and darker. She only left the house to go to work and, to top it all off, her copy of Dirty Dancing had started to jump and freeze. Even through her tear-filled, blurry vision, she could tell that Johnny was holding Baby in the air for longer than was humanly possible (even when you considered dramatic effect).

Seemingly, every tissue in existence had mopped up Claire's tears, and that included the travel packs littering her handbag. Her bin overflowing, she'd resorted to a roll of toilet paper, which now lived on her dressing table in case of emergency outbursts.

Her self-neglect and lack of care for her surroundings had reached an all-time low. Even her mother wouldn't step foot in her room. Claire remembered what she'd said: 'When life gives you lemons, Claire…'

'Yeah, all you have is a bloody bunch of lemons,' Claire muttered to herself. Whoever first uttered that quote had obviously never been through a break-up.

It wasn't as if Muscles was that big a loss, but Claire had taken it hard. Wallowing in self-pity served as a distraction and helped to fill a void – a void from not having to warm Muscles' car seat while he was in the gym, and not spending hours at the supermarket, price-checking protein bars.

Her knitting, after that day at the surgery, had been tossed into the corner of her bedroom, forgotten under a pile of dirty clothes.

Opportunities to socialise were limited to bus journeys. She knew that using public transport only proved Muscles' point that she was far from independent. In an attempt to block out such thoughts, Claire invested in an MP3 player and crammed it full of power ballads to block out the crowd every morning.

After a month of hermit-like behaviour, her parents' concern was clear. 'I want your help with the grocery shopping. I'm not taking no for an answer.' Stood in the doorway to Claire's bedroom, her mother's lips were pursed and her arms were folded tightly across her chest.

Claire groaned inwardly. She could think of nothing worse than spending her only free afternoon pushing a heavy trolley round whilst her mother flitted from aisle to aisle, in no sensible order, buying everything the family didn't need.

'It's okay, Mum, I don't need anything. Take Dad, I'm sure the newest issue of Golfing Xtreme is out today.' It was a long shot, but Claire felt she had to at least try. When she got no response she looked over at her mother and sighed. Claire knew that look well; there was no room for compromise.

At least Tuesday afternoons at the supermarket tended to be quiet. Claire took heart that she'd soon be back home as a duvet burrito. She watched her mother make her bizarre route through the store. Claire took control of the trolley and sneaked off for a few minutes down the magazine aisle. She loved to flick through the craft magazines and admire what people had created. Usually, it gave her inspiration for her own projects.

The brightly-coloured covers looked inviting. Some offered free gifts: wool, needles and trinkets every serious knitter needed. Excitedly, she scanned the selection, trying to decide which magazine to pick up first, when she heard a small cough from behind her. 'Sorry, love, can I just squeeze in there a second?'

She turned to see a petite, elderly lady pointing a bony finger at the magazine Claire was just about to reach for. As she stepped aside to let the woman past she noticed her cardigan. It was the most exquisite shade of turquoise. It draped down the old lady's back, past her hips, flattering her shape. The back panel bore intricate cable patterns and a chunky braid finished the piece off perfectly. Claire stared in awe.

To be able to create something so beautiful... Claire left quickly, after remembering the shambles that was her current knitting project. The one she'd given up on. The one collecting dust.

She rounded the corner of the fruit and vegetable aisle and heard her mother's false, high-pitched laugh, followed by a low snort. She was deep in conversation with one of the shop assistants; as Claire got closer, she realised it wasn't fresh produce they were discussing.

'Surely a strapping young man like yourself will want to

spread the fruit of your loins someday soon? As we speak, dear, all the good girls are being snapped up. And those who aren't taken…well, the clock is ticking.' Her mother winked at the guy. 'Take my Claire. Freshly single, she is, and at twenty-eight! And yet she's such a catch. She'll make a good wife to someone one day, I just know it."

'Mother!' Claire wanted the ground to swallow her up.

'Ah, here she is, my beautiful daughter. We were just talking about you.' Claire looked between her mother and the fruit and veg boy, who'd turned the same shade as the tomatoes he was holding. She needed no further explanation. 'The tills. Now!' Claire said through gritted teeth, before marching off.

She was mortified. However helpful her mother thought she was being, it had only made Claire feel even more pathetic. Now, she wouldn't be able to visit her local supermarket for fear of being asked on a date - or even worse, *not* being asked on a date! But, despite her embarrassment, the ache in her heart had come from the beautiful turquoise cardigan.

It took Lissy to put things into perspective. Claire's oldest friend, if anyone was going to get her thinking straight again, it would be Lissy. In typical style, she could be relied upon to give Claire a good old boot - or, in Lissy's case, a five-inch heel - up the backside.

Arriving home, after surviving another day of the OAP brigade at the surgery, Claire found a straight-faced, arms-crossed, foot-tapping Lissy perched on the edge of her bed. As she dropped her handbag and took off her coat, she could feel Lissy's stare burning like a good mouthwash - harsh but refreshing. Gingerly, she sat next to her friend, awaiting the onslaught. Claire made no attempt to stop Lissy's tirade; she knew she needed to hear it.

'I think it's time you and I had a talk,' said Lissy.

Claire nodded and dropped her gaze to her fidgeting hands. *Lissy would make an amazing Detective Inspector.*

'I understand that the last few weeks have been hard for you. Hell, they've probably been unbearable! But I think we're at the point now where you've got to let it go. I haven't seen or heard from you in what feels like months. You've not returned my calls, texts, or Facebook messages. And from what I've heard from your mum this evening, you've done nothing but lock yourself away up here and stew. It's not right, Claire.'

Claire could see, via her peripheral vision, Lissy's head bobbing up and down as she spoke. She couldn't think of anything to say in her defence.

Lissy continued, 'I've done some research. I know at first this may sound a little crazy, but hear me out. Break-ups can be nasty; we've all been there. But there are bad break-ups and then there's this. I know the word 'depression' gets thrown around way too loosely these days…' At that, Claire's head snapped up. 'Wait, wait, let me finish.' Lissy raised a perfectly manicured hand to stop an interruption. 'I mean it, hear me out. When you're as down as this, it can be a very slippery slope. I really think you should get some help.' Claire raised her eyebrows. 'I'm not implying we run off and get you a psychiatrist. What about self-help? I've looked at a lot of things online, and it's pretty incredible.'

Claire stared at her best friend, her eyes even wider. That Lissy thought she needed such a level of intervention was shocking enough, but that she'd used the internet for something other than make-up tutorials and internet shopping?! This was serious.

'Honestly, across the world people have published books on any subject you can think of, and how you can get through it.' Lissy listed them, using her fingers as bullet points. 'Relationship advice, marriage, sex, dieting, confidence, communication, bereavement - you name it. It's like a community who have all experienced the same problem you have, reaching out to you from the better side and offering you a massive hug. I seriously think you should look into it. I think it would help.'

Still Claire said nothing.

'If I'm honest, I'm worried about you,' said Lissy, less sternly, filling the awkward silence. 'We all are. Me, your mum, your dad…none of us like seeing you like this. But we've tried our hardest to help you, and you're not letting any of us in.' The exasperation showed on Lissy's face. 'So, now it's up to you. I know you can do it. I just think you needed someone to tell you so.' She smiled, and held her hands out for a hug, an offer that Claire instantly accepted.

Claire squeezed her friend tightly, grateful for the human contact - enjoying a warmth she didn't even know she was craving. Lissy's signature scent of soft vanilla, mixed with the zesty coconut fragrance that emanated from her long mahogany hair, tickled Claire's nose as she burrowed her face into her friend's shoulder, in a desperate attempt to stop the tears. 'Just let me know when you're ready and I'll be behind you one hundred percent of the way,' whispered Lissy. 'You've just got to take the first steps on your own. I know you can get over this.'

It was a few days later, as Claire scrambled around under her duvet for the TV remote, that she conceded Lissy was right. The time for moping around was over. She needed to get back out there, to take life by the horns and ride it like a bronco. To do that, though, she needed help, but the journey started with her. She needed the right mindset. She had to *want* to change.

Cocooned in her duvet, Claire made a promise to herself. She would emerge from all of this as a beautiful butterfly. At that exact moment of enlightenment, Claire's hands curled round the remote. Absent-mindedly, she pressed 'play', and the opening scenes of Dirty Dancing ran for the fourth time that day.

Metamorphosis starts first thing tomorrow morning…

Chapter Four

"Adventure awaits behind closed doors"

The big bookstore chain, Blurbs, had taken everything that made Cover Story, Claire's local book shop, quirky and inviting and turned it on its head. Blurbs referred to itself as the 'new look' of reading. Its décor was minimalist: uniform rows of black bookshelves surrounded by white glossy walls; it was the definition of swish. No comfy mismatched seats, small tables and quaint desk lamps tucked away in little cubby-holes; instead, Blurbs favoured sleek black leather pouffes at regular intervals - just big enough for shoppers to perch on when browsing, but not appropriate for wasting away a few hours.

Even the staff dressed in matching black and white attire, which would have been more appropriate in a jewellers', or high-end tailors'. Although they were polite and friendly, they didn't engage in chit-chat, or show any interest in the products they sold. The experience felt clinical and distant, certainly as far as book lovers were concerned.

Right now, though, Claire felt far from her comfort zone, and anonymity was what she wanted. Better than donning a ridiculous disguise, and trying to master an accent that would likely be unrecognisable to any living creature, heading out of town was the best option. Blurbs was in Berlington city centre, a twenty-minute train journey away. If anything else, it was an opportunity to get out of the house.

Lissy will be thrilled.

As the train sped along the tracks, Claire planned out where she needed to go. Berlington was a big city, and the place Muscles had always taken her when he needed more exotic protein concoctions and herbal remedies. She'd also trawled the shops there not so long ago, with Lissy, when it was absolutely *crucial* the latter got the exact dress she'd seen some big-name celebrity wearing on the television. It was where she headed for the seaweed face cream her mum adored (apparently, it was the only cream that ironed out her wrinkles without making her eyes smart). Much more importantly, Berlington was home to Claire's favourite coffee shop: The Bean and Mug. The reason why she was heading to Berlington city centre didn't really matter, as long as there was time for a coffee.

Claire glanced round the carriage. She took a moment to appreciate the array of woolly scarves and novelty bobble hats adorning her fellow passengers. Though she didn't want to think about it, she couldn't help envisaging her own knitting, still crumpled in the corner of her room. She'd tried again to pick up her disaster of a jumper; she'd even felt a glimmer of motivation when the vicar's wife saw her knitting and encouraged her to do something for their Christmas charity boxes. Within hours, Claire's project had changed from jumper to blanket, but after two evenings at war with the wool, she decided to lay it back down to rest. She gave the vicar fair warning that she couldn't fulfil her promise, though she wasn't convinced he'd understood her predicament - that the blankets were too holey.

She took a closer look at the people around her, and felt her heart ache. She appeared to be surrounded by couples. Cosy couples, giggling couples, loved-up couples. The only empty seat in the whole carriage was the one next to her. *At certain times of the year, it's truly crappy to be single.* Christmas was one of them.

She'd never really noticed how couple-orientated the festive season was, but she'd always been on the right side of things until now. *Isn't this trip supposed to be taking my mind off everything, rather than making me dwell?*

She gazed out of the window instead, just as the train hit a stretch of tunnel. In the darkness, her reflection stared back at her. She looked pale and exhausted.

Stepping onto Berlington's High Street, Claire was consumed by a flood of people coming at her from every angle.

Not one of them paused, even when they barged straight into her. Unused to the hustle and bustle and the towering buildings, she felt like a solitary drop of water in an ocean. She wrapped her forest-green duffel coat tighter around her middle and gave herself an inconspicuous hug.

You're in the big city, small town girl - remember? She put her head down to avoid the bitter wind biting at her cheeks and headed towards Blurbs.

Arriving at the store, Claire realised she had no idea what she was looking for, or to which department she should head. A spontaneous trip stemming from a sheer moment of madness (i.e. Lissy's words actually making sense) seemed to point to a wrong decision at that moment, and Claire was quickly starting to regret being there.

Panicking slightly, and lacking the confidence to tell a stranger about her specific (and highly personal) needs, Claire walked towards the giant map that showed the shop's genres and categories. She squinted at the white words on the glossy black panel, the glare of which was exacerbated by the intense lighting above.

'According to this, I need the basement,' she muttered.

She wasn't in the mood to make awkward lift chit-chat, and considering that the basement was reserved for books referencing the body and mind, Claire opted for the safer option: the stairs. *A little ironic,* she mused, *asking customers to head downhill when they're trying to pick themselves up.*

The basement was practically deserted. Appreciating the peace, Claire headed to the medical section, but as she rounded the corner she came to an abrupt halt. A man was stood in exactly the place Claire needed to be. Stood at a little over six feet tall, with a build Claire could only describe as gangly, he wore battered high-top trainers, jeans, and a grey double-breasted jacket. This ensemble was complimented by a chunky hand-knitted scarf, with moss green, mustard and plum stripes; Claire couldn't even count how many times it wound round his neck. His floppy, dark brown hair threatened to fall across his face, but the thick-rimmed glasses he wore held it back.

Claire wasn't sure if he'd noticed her. He hadn't looked up. His focus was on the book he held, which she deduced was on the subject of quitting smoking. His chiselled jaw was set straight through concentration - he was engrossed. He gripped the book so tightly his knuckles were almost white. Claire knew she was in the right place.

The self-help section was confined to the end of a book-case, which initially appeared to be full of medical encyclo-paedias and self-diagnosis guides. To effectively browse the titles in such a small space - despite the fact the guy had the proportions of a rake - meant they'd be rubbing shoulders at the very least.

Claire paused. *I can do this, I can do this, I can do this...* She repeated this mantra to herself whilst pretending to have an interest in the books on the shelf beside her.

Gathering her courage, she stole sly glances at the scarf-wearing smoker. *He's cute, in a lost sort of way, I guess. It's likely I'll knock into him, but that's no big deal. You can do this, Claire. You can handle one kind-of-cute bookworm.*

He still hadn't moved, and she couldn't walk away now. She'd acted on her crazy friend's life advice, plucked up the courage to leave the house, and travelled a fair distance; she couldn't back out because another lost soul had also found their way to the department.

Trying her best to appear casual, she stepped beside him. She took a deep breath and bent to look at the lower shelves of the section. Claire had no idea there were so many books on the subject of helping yourself. Her eyes flicked across the spines, and she debated whether each one could aid her cause.

Dieting, how to dress to suit your body shape, insomnia, grief, bereavement, trauma, stress...the list was endless. Her gaze fell on a few with the words 'relationships' in their titles. On closer inspection, it seemed they championed the saving of readers' relationships, with little advice on picking up the pieces after an explosion. No, Claire's partner hadn't kept her awake with his snoring. No, they hadn't rowed all the time, and no, the sex hadn't been bad at all (just non-existent). Claire sighed. Even the self-help books seemed to be mocking her.

Still, she continued looking, and eventually found that Lissy was right – there really was help for everyone. After advice for those in relationships came guidance for singletons. She reached for a couple of the titles and her arm brushed against the guy's leg. She'd almost forgotten he was there.

'Sorry.' She looked up sheepishly.

He momentarily lifted his gaze from the quitting smoking bible and their eyes met. Claire instantly felt her heart accelerate. It thudded so hard she could hear it in her ears.

'It's no problem,' he said.

What am I doing? This is a stranger in a bookstore. She turned her head away to break the intensity of his stare, but there was no denying the spark that still lingered in the air between them. Claire remained crouched and, on her knees, balanced the pile of books she'd somehow managed to pull from the shelf.

She flipped the top book over to read the blurb but took no notice of the words it displayed. Instead, her eyes fixed upon the guy's shoes. His feet were big but slender, perfectly matching the rest of his appearance. His trainers had seen better days: the toes were heavily scuffed and the laces were grey on the ends; one of them was in danger of becoming undone. Distracted by such details, she didn't feel the pile of books sliding from her knees until they thudded onto the floor. *Shit!*

She scrambled to pick them up, her cheeks turning pink. At the same time, the guy abandoned his read and bent down to help her. At that precise moment, Claire leant forwards for the last book and the pair bumped heads.

'Oh my God, I'm so sorry!' She lifted the remaining books skywards and jumped to her feet. The guy held out the offending title with one hand and rubbed his head with the other. Claire's cheeks deepened further, to a fetching shade of crimson. 'Oh, thanks,' she gasped. 'I mean, sorry. But thank you.' Feeling awkward, she took the book from him.

'Don't worry about it.' The guy shot Claire a crooked smile. For a moment, neither of them moved. They just stood, their gazes locked. Claire's heart began to thump again.

Just stop it, will you?! A guy smiles at you and you turn to jelly!

The books now safely in her arms, she decided the best thing to do was get out of there as quickly as possible. Without saying another word, she turned on her heel.

Despite herself, she couldn't resist taking a final glance at the bookworm. His fingers were once again locked onto the quitting smoking book. His focus was back on its pages, but his expression had changed. His eyes looked to be twinkling behind their thick black frames, and his mouth still bore that crooked smile.

Claire bit her lip and scurried towards the stairs. *Get a grip! You're twenty-eight, not twelve.*

She could still feel heat in her cheeks when she reached the next floor. She darted down the first aisle she came to; satisfied that she was out of view, Claire let herself relax a little. After taking a few deep breaths, she scanned the books beside her, to find out which department had given her refuge.

'Beginners' Knits'; 'Cast On, Cast Off', and 'Creative Cables' sat proudly on their shelf. Of all the aisles she could have stumbled into, the craft department had been her saviour. Finding herself in the knitting section was like bumping into an old friend. She felt more at ease and ran her finger along various spines, trying to decide which to pick up first.

Her mind didn't engage, however; instead, flitting back to the incident in the self-help section. She assessed the situation and decided that it hadn't been *that* bad. So she'd head-butted someone, and yes, it had been embarrassing. But it was done now - and the person in question was a stranger, someone she would probably never see again throughout her whole entire life. *A cute stranger…but still, a stranger.*

Claire sighed with relief. She continued to potter, amid the plethora of books that covered every conceivable strand of knitting and crafts. She stopped at one that was particularly eye-catching.

Intricate Intarsia. The mixture of vivid blues, purples and pinks that adorned the spine meant Claire couldn't wait to get her hands on it, and as she lifted it down to see more, she wasn't disappointed. Four women beamed at her from the cover, each wearing an expertly-knitted creation of elaborately-woven patterns. The garments appeared so tactile that Claire had to see more. She flicked through the pages and found patterns for jumpers, cardigans, waistcoats and scarves, in a rainbow of colours - each one so beautiful, it couldn't fail to turn heads.

She needed them. She felt it inside. She needed to make each and every one of those beautiful creations. To wear them with pride, because, despite her woolly shortcomings over the last month, deep down, she was a knitter. She *could* create such beauty.

Flicking forward a few pages, she checked the list of materials. Before she caught the train home, she decided, she'd visit a craft store for the necessary supplies.

Claire had never struggled with knitting patterns. She knew that, to a first-time knitter, the abbreviations could look like another language, but they'd never fazed her. As her eyes scan-read a certain pattern something happened that she'd never experienced before.

The words were there, in black and white, but nothing

made sense.

Next Row: (p1 Purple, p2 Green) to last st, p1 Purple.

Claire tried to visualise the instructions, but got her purples confused with her greens, and her p1s with her p2s. She read on, to see if it would become clearer, but it was all too quick.

Change to white, change to green, change to blue, change to purple. Knit, Purl, p2tog, K5. Change to pink, K8, change to green. Purl, Knit, Knit, Purl...

The page went blurry and Claire blinked. Her focus returned but the text still seemed unreadable. During the many years she'd been knitting, she'd taken the odd break - when life had got in the way of her hobby - but she'd always managed to pick it back up again without any effort. *Never* had it been like this. It was like she didn't know a single thing about it.

She snapped the book shut and shoved it back on the shelf, in a mixture of rage, fear and embarrassment. She quickly made for the tills and the exit. Things had gone from bad to worse, to an absolute disaster.

I need a break. Outside, she let her nose lead her towards coffee-infused salvation.

Chapter Five

"In life, there are the Go-Getters and the No-Wayers. Be a Go-Getter"

Claire looked into the velvety-rich depths of her 'salted caramel double choca-mocha'. Everything felt okay again. Life was never truly awful when she sat in her favourite corner of her favourite coffee shop, with her favourite coffee, made exactly how she liked it.

After everything that had happened, it made a change to feel pure joy. Her personal sanctuary, The Bean and Mug, held many a happy memory for Claire: girly giggles with Lissy after a long day of shopping and gossiping; coffee stops on her breaks when she was a bright-eyed student at the city college; and, of course, quiet times - when Claire stepped from life's chaos (and snatched some much-needed me-time whilst her mum yodelled away to Songs Of Praise). Every sip of her drink felt like a warm cuddle, and peace flooded through her, from the top of her head to the tips of her toes. *Bliss*.

For the first time in a long time, Claire felt like her old self. Finding the contentment she'd sought all day, she grabbed her mug and wriggled further into the plump cushions of the settee. Nothing was going to ruin the moment.

Her mocha was a pleasant mix of sweet caramel, smooth, creamy chocolate, and the bittersweet bite of coffee. She savoured the taste before taking another sip and let her eyes wander round the room. The interior of The Bean and Mug was wonderfully cosy. Comfy seats of all shapes and sizes surrounded circular, knee-height wooden tables, which created a warm, intimate atmosphere.

To Claire's left sat a man in a suit, who was leaning in far too closely to his laptop screen. The light it emitted was so powerful it made him squint; he looked like a mole. His mug sat behind the laptop, forgotten.

Across the room a young couple snuggled in 'canoodle corner' - a cubby-hole where the lighting was dimmer, and the angle of the furniture afforded a little privacy. Unfortunately for her, the position of Claire's seat meant they were in direct sight. The pair looked longingly into each other's eyes, and they held hands whilst their other hand cradled their mug. *Ugh!* It was enough to make the milk in Claire's coffee curdle. There were a few more customers dotted around but the place wasn't overly busy. She relaxed, and began to enjoy the anonymity.

Then she glimpsed someone familiar, in a seat that usually remained empty - due to the draught from the door when anyone entered or departed. Perched on the edge of the wraparound chair, his gangly limbs actively working against its design, was the guy from the bookstore. Claire's breath caught in her throat.

His eyes were glued on something outside. A storm had erupted whilst she'd been in the shopping centre, so Claire was confident that all he could see was rain.

Her cheeks threatened to flush again as she remembered her clumsiness in the book store. She tried not to dwell; instead, she took in the finer details of his appearance. Like the fact he wore his watch on the opposite arm to most people, its face on the underside of his wrist. She noted that the ends of his fringe flicked to the side, probably due to the way his hair rested on the frames of his glasses. His hands looked to be cupping his coffee mug for warmth, but no steam rose from the inside. The whole time she watched him, he never moved an inch - seemingly transfixed by the raindrops dancing down the coffee shop window.

Claire suddenly became aware of her heartbeat. Whether it was down to the amount of caffeine she'd consumed, or her euphoria at feeling like her old self again, it brought on a moment of folly.

This is a sign.

She grabbed her bag of books and pulled one out. Flicking

to a random page, under the influence of the moment, she read the chapter title: *Misery Loves Company. Exploring the difficulties of life, together.* Claire wrinkled her nose. She was on the brink of an adventure into the realms of self-help, and already she'd hit a brick wall.

'In our darkest hours as humans, we find ourselves at our most vulnerable. During times of complete despair and heartbreak it can be very easy to feel alone and isolated from society. It can feel as if we're in our own little bubble, one that no one can burst.'

Claire looked at the guy across the room, who was still staring vacantly through the window. *Was* he *in his own little bubble?*

She read on. *'Sometimes, it can be hard to interact with people who are not going through the same things as we are. When people do not understand one's emotional state, it can be very hard to communicate on the same level, without it feeling false or awkward. That's why I have come to believe so strongly in the theory that misery loves company. Who better to turn to in our darkest of times than someone who's experiencing the exact same thing?'*

Claire broke away from the page again. Although he wasn't facing her, she could see the guy's reflection quite clearly. He appeared pale and washed out, and his lips made a hard, straight line. His eyes seemed empty as he stared into the distance.

Quitting smoking is obviously taking its toll, because he looks bloody miserable.

She shut the book and took a moment to fully digest the words. It was almost as if the book was telling her to go over and make a friend; that the guy from the bookstore could be the answer to her problems.

But who does that? Who marches over and introduces themselves to a complete stranger? Especially one they'd bumped heads with only an hour ago.

It was absolute lunacy. *He'd call security if I did, surely?* She placed the book on the table. *This whole self-help thing is nonsense.*

She returned her attention to her double choca-mocha, but couldn't stop her gaze flitting between the book and the guy. Then she focused on the empty seat opposite him.

Does misery really love company?

She felt the need to prove something, though she wasn't entirely sure what. She rose from her chair and tucked the book under her arm. 'Watch this! I'll show you how much misery loves company!' she muttered, as she made her way across the room.

She reached his table, but to her dismay, he continued to stare through the window. It took the horrid scraping sound of chair against floor before his attention was caught.

She sat opposite him. 'Hi. You may not, um, remember me...' Claire began. '...or maybe you do. I'm the woman from Blurbs. The lady you bumped heads with earlier.'

He didn't say a word. He seemed startled. Claire cleared her throat. 'Well, I just wanted to say...seeing as we were both at that same section, I, er, understand you're suffering right now. So, I thought I'd come and ask you how you were getting on... It must be tough trying to break a habit. How long has it been since your last cigarette?'

The guy remained mute, but his expression changed - a mix of confusion and bemusement. She could see his lips quivering, but didn't know if he was about to laugh, or question her sanity. For a brief moment, Claire feared she'd made a huge mistake.

She was about to apologise and excuse herself when he spoke. 'I've never...' he began, then corrected himself, '...I mean, I haven't smoked in years.'

Claire was confused. She could have sworn it was a 'how to quit smoking' book she'd seen him clinging onto. And it was definitely the same guy - he was still wearing that hand-knitted, never-ending scarf. But she wasn't here for small talk; she was here to prove her stupid book wrong. She decided to cut to the chase. 'The main reason I came over was to prove something to myself. You look pretty much how I've been feeling recently, so you're the perfect example. You see, this book here…' She brought it out from under her arm and laid it on the table. '…it says misery loves company, and I've been sitting over there, completely disagreeing with that idea.

'I was just wondering if you could help me prove that misery, in fact, does not love company. That me sitting with you is an intrusion, and I'm annoying you when all you want to be is down, miserable and alone.' Claire paused to gauge his reaction. He took a moment, which left an awkward silence hanging in the air.

'You came over to prove a book wrong?' The corners of his lips twitched as he spoke, Claire noted. And when he stopped, they sprung into the most adorable smile she'd ever seen.

She'd come this far, she couldn't back out now, so she nodded. His smile turned into a goofy grin.

'And now you're not even miserable anymore, because you're smiling. So, I'm just completely wrong, and this is really awkward. I look like a complete lunatic who talks to books and accosts complete strangers. Excuse me, I'm so sorry to have wasted your time.'

She rose, but scarf guy raised his hand to stop her. 'Hey, it's the first time I've smiled in a while. So, thank you. In fact, if you've got time for another drink I might take you up on that offer of company.'

His eyes were blue, a beautiful baby blue. 'If misery was a crucial part of your experiment, though, I'll understand if you say no.' His adorable grin never budged.

Claire was thrown. She'd expected to be ignored, ridiculed, or even sworn at for her intrusion. She hadn't reckoned on a conversation, let alone an offer of a drink. But if she was honest, the company would be welcome. She had the time to spare, and scarf guy was cute, so why not?

She accepted his offer and he soon returned with two large mugs and a little more colour to his cheeks.

And that was the day Claire met Adrian. Adrian Harwell, a tea-drinking, twenty-nine-year-old single man who lived and worked in a little village called Rosworth, on the outskirts of Berlington. As they chatted, she learned that he had his own business, and he lived alone in a bungalow. He'd been in The Bean and Mug that day for the same reason as Claire: because he'd needed a break.

'So, what's your business?' she asked.

Adrian looked at her shyly over the top of his mug. 'You promise not to laugh?' Claire nodded. 'I own a shop called Oddballs.'

A smile crept onto her lips.

'Hey! You promised,' he protested, though he smiled too.

'Sorry. What exactly does Oddballs do?'

'It's a wool shop.'

Claire almost choked on her salted caramel double cho-ca-mocha.

Chapter Six

"Where you find honesty, you will also find trust"

It was unlike Claire to be the first to arrive at The Bean and Mug, but she was just happy to get the drinks in for once. Whilst she waited, she grabbed a napkin and scribbled 'Happy Belated Christmas!' on it before tucking it under Adrian's mug.

This year, Christmas for Claire had been an annoyance. How dare it come along and interrupt the blossoming friendship between herself and Adrian?! She thought it rather rude, and she'd been more than eager for this day to arrive.

Nestled in her bag was the ball of red wool she'd grown to hate, together with her needles and the few rows of knitting that had refused to cooperate whenever she dared try. Ever since she'd found out about Adrian's wool shop, she'd longed to open up about her knitting. But how could she boast about her previous accomplishments when, currently, she could barely handle a stitch? What she stowed away in her bag wasn't a patch on what she was usually capable of. *Maybe I should ask Adrian for his advice…*

'Sorry I'm late, the traffic was horrendous. Must be all the Christmas returns.' Adrian grinned at her as he took off his coat and settled down in the chair opposite. He looked at the mug and napkin and smiled. 'Thank you. How was it for you?'

'Good, thanks. A bit strange spending so much time alone with my parents. But a good strange, if that makes any sense. How about you?'

'Another quiet one. I'll be glad when the world starts moving again. This season is a wool shop owner's dream. I've so many ideas, so many plans. It's going to be busy, but exciting!'

'When does Oddballs reopen?'

'Monday.' Adrian beamed. 'In fact, that brings me to what I wanted to ask you.' Claire shot Adrian a quizzical look, but let him continue. 'I remember you saying you used to love knitting, so I thought you might like to visit my shop. Help you rekindle your passion, perhaps?'

Claire paused. This was her chance to confess, to introduce the demon living in her handbag and start the road to knitting recovery, one stitch at a time. Instead, she nudged her bag further under the table.

'You're welcome any day, but I recommend Tuesdays,' he said.

'Why Tuesdays?'

'You'll see.' Adrian's grin just increased Claire's curiosity.

*

A week later, Claire was waiting at a bus stop in Rosworth when a rusting, snow-white Micra with a rattling exhaust pulled up to the kerb and tooted its horn. She stooped to check the identity of the driver and saw Adrian grinning back at her through the window, beckoning her inside. 'Hello, Hot Wheels,' Claire giggled as she settled herself in the passenger seat.

'Hey! This is the most reliable car I've ever known.' Adrian stroked the steering wheel. 'Were you expecting something different?'

Claire grinned. 'To be completely honest, no.'

Within minutes they parked up and made their way down the main road. Suddenly, Adrian said, 'Here we are.' He pointed to a shop in their path that was sandwiched between an estate agent and a hairdressing salon.

'Welcome to my wool shop.' He pulled a handful of jangling metal from his pocket and selected a large, ornate brass key. This, he put in the large ornate brass lock, before pressing down on the handle. But the door didn't budge, so he stepped back and gave it a shove with his hip.

He then darted inside to calm the alarm. Claire waited for the siren to cease before stepping inside.

He reappeared. 'I've just got to pop upstairs and set everything up,' he said. 'Feel free to take a look around.' He flicked a switch before heading upstairs. The lights in the shop began to flicker as they warmed up.

Throughout Claire's obsession with knitting, she'd only ever encountered one style of wool shop. On the outskirts of Dovedon, next to one of the large industrial estates, sat the Beech Bridge shopping complex, which was the home of Crafty Life. Crafty Life catered for every crafting need, all under one roof. Products were lined up in rows, each aisle displaying its own speciality; every item was catalogued and in its rightful place. The shop had a regimented feel, and with at least a ten-strong workforce, it was easy for craft lovers to feel isolated - and just plain ordinary - inside its walls.

As you browsed, no one asked about what you were making; nobody cared whether that particular shade of green wool you'd chosen would complement your eyes; and nobody ever worried if you'd picked the right dye lot. When Claire had tried to visualise Adrian's wool shop she'd pictured something similar to Crafty Life's uncomfortably large building, their overpowering artificial lights, and the excitable children inhabiting the Play-Doh aisle.

So it was a surprise, as she stood in Oddballs' doorway, to see the flickering bulbs illuminate numerous shelves that were full of brightly-coloured wool balls, all plump and fluffy, and in every colour: aquas, pinks, yellows, greens, reds, oranges and purples. She itched to touch them. It looked like there was wool everywhere, from floor to ceiling and wall to wall, organised by brand, weight and colour; each in their own little pigeon-hole with a yellow cardboard star displaying the relevant details and price.

Displays were far from uniform. Shelving was made up of a mish-mash of various woods alongside plastic units. In the middle of the room, baskets bulged with even more wool: frilly balls, furry balls, chunky balls, skinny balls.

At the back of the room was a large, round pine table with multiple chairs. It sported an array of knitted cushions and two plastic tubs that were full of ring-binders, which contained knitting patterns of all categories.

Beside the till sat a cage, housing row upon row of tubes that brimmed with various buttons. Each tube had one of the buttons it contained fastened to the lid as an example.

Behind the till area was a wall full of knitting accessories: needles, stitch markers, row counters, tape measures, pins, scissors, etc., all bearing unusual patterns and cute designs. It was enough to make her drool.

Adrian returned and found Claire in the middle of shop, drinking everything in, with her lips slightly parted in awe. He gave a small cough.

'It's like Aladdin's cave in here,' she said appreciatively.

He nodded. 'I'm glad it still offers a sense of wonder.'

The morning flew by. She learned about winter-time projects, which featured such things as thick baby blankets, chunky-knit ponchos and fluorescent bobble hats; she helped pick out wool, buttons and ribbons for multiple WIPs (Works In Progress) and UFOs (Unfinished Objects).

Claire was in her element. In the space of just a few hours she'd learned so much about a world she thought she knew well - and one she thought she'd lost. In fact, she took some convincing it was lunchtime when Adrian sat her down in the upstairs office and gave her a hot pork sandwich.

'So, how are you finding it?' Adrian asked before taking his first bite.

'Mmm, it's delicious.' Claire licked her lips without taking her eyes off the sandwich.

Adrian laughed. 'The sandwiches are good. What I meant was, how's your day going? Is it okay? Fancy picking up some needles again?'

'Oh.' Claire began to reply then realised she had her mouth full. She swallowed and nodded enthusiastically. 'It's great, I've never known anything like it. Honestly, it's amazing.' She stopped short of answering his second question.

Adrian smiled at the compliment. He focused on his food and the pair fell into an easy silence.

'I should warn you,' he said, once they'd both finished, 'we have the pleasure of some of my favourite ladies this afternoon.' Claire must have looked startled, because he added, 'Don't worry. It's just my 'Knit and Natter' group.'

At precisely two o'clock, the shop door opened and four sweet old ladies walked in. They pushed brightly-coloured happy-shopper trolleys that all overflowed with wool and needles. The room began to smell of lavender and posh soap. Claire relaxed.

'You've brought your motors today, girls, I see. I'll have to get you all a parking space,' Adrian joked. He pulled a couple of the baskets aside to allow the ladies past. As each one squeezed through, they cooed at him or affectionately patted his arm before making their way to the large round table at the back of the shop. The last lady spotted Claire and stopped to take a better look, squinting at her through lilac-tinted glasses.

'So, you're the reason Adie's had a big smile on his face recently. I might have known there'd be a girl involved.' She winked at Adrian and Claire saw him blush.

'You Knit and Natter ladies are Adrian's favourite girls, so I've heard.' Claire smiled back at the kind old face peering at her.

'Eh? Knit and Natter ladies? Oh, Adie, why did you say that? Sorry, love, we don't 'Knit and Natter' - we 'Stitch and Bitch'. We're the Bitches!'

The four of them erupted into laughter. Adrian quickly changed the subject. 'Claire, this is Gladys, Doreen, Beryl and Rene.'

'That's us! And we take our knitting *very* seriously,' said Gladys.

'I'm sure you do,' agreed Claire.

'No, we really do. I'll show you.' Gladys began rolling up her sleeve in an attempt to reveal her upper-arm but she couldn't get the fabric high enough. Beryl lent a hand, pulling at the sleeve until it lifted.

On Gladys' arm was a tattoo. Claire tried her hardest not to laugh as she leaned in for a closer look. It was quite a detailed image, consisting of a ball of red wool with two knitting needles menacingly jabbed through the centre, in the style of a skull and crossbones. Above this image were three words: *Knit Or Dye*.

'Um, that's...' Claire searched for the appropriate word, '... lovely.'

'You think that's good, take a look at these!' Gladys brandished her fists under Claire's nose. The word '*Knit*' was scrawled across the knuckles of one hand, with '*Wit*' on the other. 'Good, eh? I had such a giggle getting these done. Who needs love or hate when you have knitting, that's what I say.' Again, the four erupted into laughter.

Eventually, they fished out their woollen projects from their bags - a clear signal that chit-chat was over. It was time to knit.

Claire watched their session, fascinated by each knitter; each one had something different on their needles. Gladys was knitting an enormous square of grey tweed, whilst Rene was creating a tiny square in lemon. Doreen's wool was as wispy as a cloud; fine and dainty, it looked like intricate lace draped across her needles. Beryl's wool was thick, chunky, and bright green, and she seemed to be shaping it into a hat of some description. Claire admired the different projects and techniques at play and wished that she could pick up her needles and join them.

More than once she caught Adrian looking at her. She'd catch his eye then look away, like she was doing something she shouldn't.

At half-time, Claire offered to make the ladies a coffee. When she returned with a tea-tray that bore everyone's preferred brew, she found that a chair had been pulled up for her.

'Take a seat, luvvie.' Gladys patted the empty seat. 'We don't bite, I promise.'

Claire sat down then spotted Adrian grinning. *So, this was his plan all along.*

'Have you ever fancied yourself as a knitter, Claire?' asked Beryl, as she finally laid down her knitting in favour of her coffee cup.

'Oh yes.' Claire nodded enthusiastically. 'I've always loved knitting. It was one of the things me and my grandma used to do on Sunday afternoons. She created the most beautiful things. I made it my aim to become a knitter just like her.'

'And did you?' said Beryl.

'Almost.' Claire gave a wistful smile.

'Well, why didn't you say?' said Gladys. 'Let's get you some needles and wool and get you cast on.' She rose from her seat.

'Oh no, it's okay,' Claire protested. 'I'm, er, taking a break from knitting at the moment.'

The Bitches all looked at each other.

'A break?' Beryl made Claire's decision sound like the most absurd thing she'd ever heard.

'No-one takes a break from knitting,' said Gladys. 'What happened? Did you lose your pattern?'

'Did you get a really big knot in your wool?' said Beryl.

'Did you break a needle?' offered Rene.

'Did you become frustrated because of an abbreviation that wasn't clear?' added Doreen with a nod.

'No, no.' Claire hesitated. If she was going to tell anyone about her knitting woes it would be the Bitches. But how to put it… When she ran through the words in her head, it sounded crazy.

'It's just that, at the moment, every time I pick up my needles, I just… *can't.*' No one spoke and Claire began to feel awkward. She wished she'd never said anything, and debated leaving the table.

'There's no such word as can't, dear,' said Rene quietly. 'If it's not a physical hurdle then it'll be an emotional one. Until you figure out which, you're going to struggle. But you'll get there. It may just be a case of mind over matter.' She patted Claire's hand.

'If you do figure it out, or want to try again,' Gladys added, 'you know where we are. We'd love to have you, wouldn't we, ladies?' There was a chorus of approval.

'Thank you,' said Claire, touched by their words. 'You do take your knitting seriously, don't you?' The Bitches nodded.

Around 4pm, the Bitches packed up. After rifling through the new yarns - and buying a bag full each, despite their already-overflowing trolleys – they departed, toddling off in their separate directions.

'Are my ears playing tricks on me, or did I hear you say that you can't knit?' Adrian locked the shop door and flipped the knitted 'open' sign over, so that it read 'closed'.

'What's this, a woolly lock in?' Claire laughed, but he didn't reply. She sighed. 'Yes, you heard right.' A frown formed on Adrian's face. 'I used to be able to knit really well. But, lately, well…I just can't. I'm sure it's just a phase. I'll get over it soon enough.' She dismissed the issue with a flick of her hand, but a lump formed in her throat.

'Well,' Adrian shrugged, 'if you want to stick around, I'm sure the Bitches will be more than happy to help you rediscover your talent.'

It was Claire's turn to frown. 'I thought *you* were the knitting master? Why can't you help me?'

'Because I believe the problem isn't with the knitting, but with the knitter.'

'Try telling that to my unruly needles!' Claire laughed, but inside she squirmed. He'd hit a nerve. She sat back at the table while Adrian cashed up, to collect her thoughts. She cast off a knitted garment.

'You know, I was scared about bringing you here today,' admitted Adrian. 'But it's definitely worked out for the best.'

'What do you mean? This place is amazing!'

He took a long look around the shop, as if seeing it for the first time. 'I know that,' he said quietly, 'I was scared I would lose you.' He choked a little on the word 'lose', as if it didn't belong in the sentence.

'What do you mean, 'lose me'? Surely I don't blend in with this many colours?' Claire smiled and gestured to the various hues.

'No, not in that way. You'd have had to wear one hell of an outfit to achieve that! No, it's just that I try to keep my work and my...' He paused. 'My friends separate, and you've kind of blurred that boundary today.'

Claire was confused. *If I owned a place like this I'd show it off to everyone.*

She heard him take a deep breath. 'Two years ago, I thought I would go under. The takings hit an all-time low, and my social life reached a peak. I had to make a choice: work or play - and I couldn't let my mother down. Ever since then, I eat, sleep and breathe Oddballs.

'Don't get me wrong, I love this place. I love the business and I love the people. But when I found you, I had the seeds of a social life again. I had something to look forward to besides business meetings and deliveries. Then, when you said you had an interest in knitting, I realised it would have been cruel of me to not bring you here. I'm your friend, and I'm also an avid knitter; if there's one thing I want to do it's to help you rekindle your love for the craft. I can't let you lose faith in your hobby when I run a place like this. I just don't want it to change anything between us.'

Claire's mind swam with a million questions; she felt that if she didn't share them immediately, her head might explode. But, after seeing Adrian's face, she decided to keep quiet. She could always find out more later.

Instead, she shook her head and smiled sweetly. 'It won't.'

In the car on the way home one question would not go away. When there was a lull in their small talk, Claire couldn't help herself. 'So, come on, what made you decide you wanted to own a wool shop?'

'I'm surprised you've waited so long to ask me that,' he said. 'It's normally the first question on everyone's lips.' Claire quietly breathed a sigh of relief that she'd not offended him. 'Oddballs was my mother's business. After my dad walked out on her, she felt like all her dreams had been crushed. But no one could take her knitting away from her. She compounded all her sadness and anger, and used that energy to start her own business. I must admit, at the beginning, it was stressful and slow, but with some care and appreciation word got round. Everyone knew my mother as 'the crazy knitting lady who runs the wool shop down the road'. Pretty much as soon as I could talk we became business partners. 'Knitted together' - that's what people used to say about us.'

He looked distant, as if he was somewhere else. 'I can still see her now, standing behind the till, all smiles and cable-knit jumpers. Some of my happiest memories feature Oddballs; I've probably spent as much of my life there as I have at home.'

She noticed his whimsical look change to sadness. 'Her death was quite long and drawn out. I should have been ready for it; she continually warned me from the moment she was diagnosed as terminal. But when it happened, I wasn't prepared. Nothing seemed real. For weeks, I waited for her get back from whatever daft business adventure she'd been on, so she could fill me in on all the new fashions and yarns. But that day never came.'

'I'm so sorry, Adrian,' said Claire.

'It's okay.' He looked across at her and smiled before turning back to the road. 'So, to answer your question, Mum left me the house, the shop, the business, everything. I was just twenty-three and a business owner. I thought I was the bees' knees! When life got a bit easier I took advantage; I changed the shop's opening hours to accommodate my social life. I'd miss deliveries and cancel reps' appointments, just so I could knock off early and get to a party. And Odd-balls suffered as a result. I was immature, and I almost paid a huge price for my stupidity. It's only been this last twelve months or so that things have started to get back on track.'

He paused at the end of the road until a space appeared for him to pull out from the junction. 'There was one par-ticular day when I thought I was going to lose it all, and at that point I made a vow that I would never let it happen. I lost contact with my friends – none of them bothered with me once the free lifts stopped and they didn't have a place to kip. But that just goes to show they didn't really matter. I know I've done the right thing.'

Claire, unsure of how to comfort someone when they were driving, placed her hand on Adrian's knee and squeezed gently.

'When you saw me that day in Blurbs, I'll be honest, I wasn't searching for a book on quitting smoking. I was after some information that could help me with my finances. I've kicked the bad habits but the damage is still there, and I won't rest until it's completely fixed. I planned never to have a social life ever again. Until you came along...' Adrian barely spoke those final words, but Claire still heard them.

'No wonder you were confused when I came over and started asking you about your cigarette habit!' Claire laughed in an attempt to lighten the mood. 'Why didn't you just tell me the real reason?'

'I didn't want you to think of me as a failure.'

'I was a stranger in a bookstore, why did it matter?'

'Hey, a man can dream, can't he?' Claire looked at him and saw the twinkle in his eyes.

They drove on, making small talk and chatting about their

day. Adrian began to describe Ponton, the village he lived in, and how close the community was.

But Claire's brain was in overdrive. She tried desperately to process everything he'd told her, in the hope of arriving at a solution.

Eventually, they pulled up outside her parents' house. 'You know your mum would be proud of you, don't you?'

He nodded. 'I know. She would be incredibly proud of me, and what I've achieved. I just think she'd be upset about what I've sacrificed in the process.'

Chapter Seven

"There is never truly a wrong or right way to go about life"

A week later the bell above the door of Oddballs chimed loudly as Claire sped in and announced, 'I have a plan!'

'Why, hello,' Adrian chuckled as he stepped down from the counter. 'What plan is this, dare I ask?'

Claire grinned. 'I've been thinking about it all week and I've got a solution. I had to come and tell you straightaway!'

Adrian's smile dropped slightly and she saw a hint of confusion across his face. 'A solution for what?'

'For our social failures! All I need is a computer, internet access, and a picture of your face.'

'I'm intrigued.' He looked at his watch. 'Let me finish up here and we'll go to my place, where you can tell me more about this crazy plan of yours. Wait in the car if you like.' He tossed Claire his keys.

Claire felt a little overwhelmed. Muscles had *never* left her with his car keys. She carried them to Adrian's car in a vice-like grip.

She'd been friends with Adrian for just over a month, and wasn't sure if she was ready for such responsibility. She popped the keys on the dashboard and sat on her hands, scared to touch anything in case her inherent clumsiness showed its face (despite an open packet of Werther's Originals in the cup-holder tempting her otherwise). A few minutes later, Adrian climbed into the driver's seat.

'You passed the test, then.' Claire looked at him, puzzled. 'You didn't drive off into the sunset, which means you're not a complete lunatic. I feel safer about allowing you into my home.' He winked. 'I had to check!'
Claire elbowed him in the side as he started the engine.

On the way, Claire tried to picture Adrian's house. At first, she imagined a stereotypical bachelor pad, or 'man den', but remembering Adrian's vow of all work and no play, she changed her mind. *A minimalist environment!* White and black, with perhaps a few business papers, books and folders scattered around. Just the bare necessities and maybe a few mod-cons. He'd said himself, he spent most of his life at the shop and not at home.

As they pulled onto the drive, Claire couldn't believe her eyes. A quaint little bungalow greeted her, like a scaled-down model of a suburban cottage. She adored it already. Ivy covered part of the property, and a cute little chimney sat in the middle of the roof. Every window was leaded in a diamond design. All that was missing was a white picket fence.

Adrian unlocked the door and gestured for her to go inside. On one side of the hall was a floor-to-ceiling ma-hogany bookcase, housing row upon row of books, every colour and size. As she got closer, she gasped; they weren't just any old books, they were all craft books. Topics covered knitting, crochet, dress-making and sewing; there were books on baking, painting and jewellery craft…a lifetime's worth of hobbies stacked up. Not a single business folder or accounting book in sight.

'This place is beautiful,' Claire whispered. Adrian smiled as he took her jacket and hung it on the antique coat-stand.

He led her into the living room, where she took note of the various homely touches. Every flat surface was covered in a delicate hand-crocheted doily; it was like a scattering of oversized snowflakes. Numerous vases held a range of flower arrangements in pretty muted colours, and on the walls hung exquisite cross-stich samplers, each perfectly finished with a mount and frame.

'You've a lovely home,' Claire sighed.

'My mother's doing,' said Adrian. 'She had a way of mak-ing a place feel like home.'

While Adrian disappeared to gather what they needed for 'the plan', Claire spotted a number of photo frames on the wall; a bright, smiling face shone out from every one. A snapshot of time during birthday celebrations and family Christmases; pictures of famous landmarks and snaps taken by the sea. Claire even spotted Adrian as a baby amongst the photos; he was snuggled under a hand-knitted blanket. His chubby cheeks and wrinkled nose made her smile. *Perfect moments captured and preserved.*

'That's my mum.' She didn't know Adrian was behind her until he spoke. He gestured to a photo of a woman sporting a multi-coloured woolly jumper. She had a wild mass of dark brown hair and a beautiful smile. Claire couldn't help but smile back at her.

'And this must be you.' Claire pointed to the baby in the lady's arms.

Adrian nodded. 'There you go. You said you needed a picture of my face.'

Claire laughed. 'We might need one a little more recent than that.' She noticed that Adrian's laptop had appeared on the coffee table, along with two steaming mugs; one coffee, one tea.

'Right then,' said Claire, sitting on the sofa. 'We best get started.' She'd almost forgotten about her masterplan, distracted by Adrian's picturesque home. She gently placed her mug on one of the intricate doilies. 'When we boil everything down to the simplest explanation, the common factor that features in both our problems is relationships, or a distinct lack thereof. I mean, look at us! We're both on the wrong side of twenty and painfully single.' Adrian nodded. 'I've forgotten what it's like to be single, let alone date again, and you've completely dismissed any notion of a relationship. My parents were married by the time they were our age.'

Claire saw Adrian visibly freeze. 'I, um, I'm getting ahead of myself,' she added. 'What I'm trying to say is that we need to find love, and I think I've found a way.'

Adrian nodded a little more enthusiastically and she saw that twinkle in his eye yet again. 'Okay,' he agreed. 'But why do we need the laptop and picture?'

'I thought it was obvious. I've done some research, and statistics show that twenty percent of relationships now start from online dating. So, what are we waiting for?' She looked at Adrian excitedly but he seemed crestfallen.

Confused, she continued to explain. 'There's one called 'FishTank', and they claim to have 'all the fish you need in one tank'. We just create a profile, fill in a few details, add a photo and voilà! We'll be dating the people of our dreams in no time, and it's all just a few clicks away!'

Adrian still didn't look impressed. 'I thought you meant...'

Claire interrupted, a little disappointed that Adrian was nowhere near as thrilled as she was. 'Sorry if I confused you. I was just excited, I probably didn't explain myself properly. But what do you think? Do you fancy giving it a go? I will if you will.' She smiled expectantly, but Adrian still seemed unsure.

After some gentle coaxing and the bribe of a Chinese takeaway, he eventually agreed. A few moments later, the website was loaded and Claire tried to stop her hands from shaking with excitement. As she readied the camera on her phone, Adrian polished his glasses.

'Ready for your photoshoot, Mr Harwell?' Claire giggled as she watched Adrian fidget with his glasses, then his fringe, then his cardigan. He managed to finish preening, and Claire, as if she'd been doing it all her life, clicked a few buttons on her camera. 'All done.'

Adrian blinked. 'But I wasn't even ready!'

'It's all about the natural shots these days. No one wants to date a poser.' Adrian rolled his eyes but seemed happy that his time under the spotlight was through.

'My turn.' Adrian reached for the phone as Claire straightened her jumper and flattened her hair. There was a sudden burst of light and Claire glared at Adrian.

'What?' Adrian tried to look innocent, but he couldn't

hide his mischievous grin. 'I thought it was all about the natural shot.' Claire shook her head and posed, this time ready for the flash.

After the hundredth photo Adrian lowered the camera. 'Honestly, Claire, there are some lovely shots here. I'm sure you can find one you're happy with.' He joined her on the sofa.

There were a few moments of silence while the photos were scrutinised. 'Oh, Adrian!' Claire grumbled. 'You've cut half my head off!'

'People aren't going to be interested in the top of your head. I got the face bit in.' She switched her phone to selfie mode and posed again for a better photo. At the crucial moment, Adrian leaned over and bobbed his tongue out. The picture flashed up on the screen and she giggled. A succession of snaps followed, with Adrian pulling silly faces in the background and Claire laughing so much she couldn't breathe. She shoved him away to order the food and managed to capture a few sensible shots.

As they ate, the pair considered the profile questions on the site, and debated which answers would impress. Claire's heart melted when Adrian declared that his 'perfect first date' would be a picnic at a drive-thru movie, and he looked impressed when Claire revealed her 'hidden talent' was touching her nose with her tongue and wiggling her ears at the same time.

By the end of the night, they'd successfully set up their dating profiles. As Adrian switched off the laptop, Claire felt like a child on Christmas Eve, anticipating the results of their hard work in the morning. They agreed to keep each other informed and, with a contented smile, a belly full of tasty Chinese food, and a sense of accomplishment, Claire asked Adrian to take her home.

Back in her bedroom after Adrian had dropped her off, Claire couldn't resist getting out her laptop. She reassessed their evening's work; everything seemed fine…apart from her photo.

My cheeks look puffy and my skin is too pale. She scrutinised every inch of the picture, but the thing that bothered her the most was the way her eyes looked blank and empty. She picked up her phone and swiped through the photos from that evening. All the ones on her own, she hated. There was always something wrong, no matter how small or picky the issue. Then she reached the ones she'd taken when Adrian was messing around. Her smile was genuine; she was radiant, natural.

She lingered on them for a little while, then changed her profile picture to one of those, cropping the image so that only a chunk of Adrian's shoulder and a spike of his dark brown hair could be seen.

Chapter Eight

"Act upon the golden opportunities when they arise. Don't let a good thing just pass you by"

At work the next day, Claire's usual backing track of coughs and grunts throughout the surgery was interrupted by the trill of her mobile phone. She glanced into her knitting bag; Adrian's name flashed up on the screen.

As inconspicuously as she could, she scooped up her phone. *Hey Clairebear87!!! Guess who just got a like on their photo and a 'Hi' in their inbox! A X*

Claire froze. Less than twenty-four hours into their Fish-Tank experience Adrian had been contacted, whilst Claire's inbox was gathering cyber-dust. She felt a prickle of jealousy, but her curiosity drew her on. Besides, this had been her idea, so she should show some support.

She replied: *Oi, Oddball101! Clairebear87 is trying to work :P But, that's great news! Meet me tomorrow at The Bean and Mug, 1.30pm, for coffee and details. Xx*

At The Bean and Mug the next day, Claire heard the full story. The 'Hi' in Adrian's inbox was from 'Abiii_xxx'. Her profile picture showed a petite blonde, and, from the way Adrian scrolled down his phone screen, lines of text blurring as he went, Claire could tell that the 'Hi' in Adrian's inbox had escalated quickly. In short, Abiii xxx had asked Adrian on a date and he'd agreed.

'So, when's your hot date with *Abiiiiii?*" Claire wasn't exactly sure where the sarcastic tone to her voice had come from, but Adrian appeared oblivious.

'Tomorrow night.'

Claire thought her eyes might pop out of her skull. 'Tomorrow night? Adrian! Why didn't you say?' In a snap, Claire's jealous grump vanished. It's okay to be a little sulky when your friend is doing way better than you at something, she reasoned (especially when that something was your idea in first place), but it's not okay to let your friend walk blindly into a situation that could potentially mess up. Jealousy or no jealousy, Claire couldn't let him go on the date unprepared.

'You've changed your tune,' he said. 'What's wrong with tomorrow?'

'Nothing's wrong, it's just soon.'

Claire saw Adrian's cheeks colour slightly. 'I know, she couldn't wait.'

She felt sick, but held it together. She wanted to be a good friend, so she gave Adrian his orders. 'Get ready at my house - I won't take no for an answer. Bring a selection of outfits, some aftershave, and any worries you have. We can settle it all before you go.'

'Yes, ma'am.' He saluted playfully, but a second later added, 'Thank you. Help would be great. Dates for me are something that became extinct with the dinosaurs.'

Claire smiled. Adrian really was adorable sometimes.

The following evening, there was a timid knock on Claire's parents' front door. Claire had been sat on the stairs, waiting, and opened the door before Adrian lowered his arm.

'Hi.' A grin appeared on Adrian's face the moment he saw her.

Claire smiled back, but her face fell as she looked Adrian up and down. His hair had taken a beating from the vicious wind and his fringe flopped in his face. His never-ending scarf had slipped and one side almost trailed along the floor. And, as she looked downwards, she saw he had on those awful trainers.

'Please tell me you remembered a selection of outfits.'

'They're in the boot.' He turned back to his car and she followed, praying he'd brought a change of shoes.

Claire had pre-warned her parents that a new male friend would be visiting that evening. In the style of a pubescent teen, she'd made them promise to stay out of the way.

Adrian was just a friend, she'd stressed, but a new friend, and she didn't want him scared away by their intrusive, potentially inappropriate, and most certainly embarrassing questions.

For the most part, they kept their promise.

In Claire's room, after banishing Adrian's scarf from outfit to bag, she assessed the three selections he'd brought. As she did so, he explored the little oddments, knick-knacks and treasures Claire had on her shelves: tiny photo frames housing even tinier photographs, thimbles from across the world, keyrings, painted pebbles, glass ornaments and ticket stubs. He admired each of them in turn.

Claire was quite impressed with Adrian's choices. He'd brought a couple of different shirts and had teamed them with a navy-blue slim-fit blazer and dark skinny jeans. *Not too formal but with an air of sophistication.* The only decision was which colour shirt to go with: crisp white, red check or ice blue. As she deliberated, she asked a question, knowing she didn't really want to hear the answer. 'Have you booked a table?'

'Yep. I managed to get table for two at The Trout at High Tide.'

Claire shook her head. *Trust him to pick a restaurant with the word 'trout' in the title for a first date!* Of all the words in the English dictionary, 'trout' did not conjure up romance. But he seemed chuffed with his choice and Claire had heard good reviews about the place.

She settled on the blue shirt and sent Adrian with a tub of hair wax to the bathroom.

He eventually emerged. The iciness of his shirt picked up the piercing blue of his eyes perfectly, and his clothes hugged his slender frame in all the right places. His after-shave cut through the air; a little strong, but musky. He'd used the wax as per Claire's instructions, to tame his fringe neatly to the side, away from the rim of his glasses, which showed off those eyes and that strong jaw-line to maximum effect.

Claire's heart quickened.

Then she looked down, and saw that he was *still* wearing those damned trainers.

'Hold on a second.' She disappeared downstairs.

Murmurs of an exchange between Claire and her parents floated up the stairs; then the sound of a few doors opening, more murmurs, and Claire calling his name. He made his way into the living room where the whole family waited.

Claire presented him with a pair of leather slip-on dress shoes. They proved one size too big, so he was also presented with a pair of knitted socks - an unworn Father's Day present from the previous year, she explained. Adrian looked at the socks and threw Claire a quizzical look. They were knitted perfectly; there wasn't a single stitch out of place.

'T-thank you,' Adrian stammered as he gratefully accepted the shoes and sat down on the sofa to put them on.

'It's no problem, boy.' Claire's father replied, despite his promise to stay silent. 'So where are you taking my daughter this evening?'

Adrian spluttered. Claire jumped in hurriedly. 'He's, er, not taking me anywhere, Dad. Adrian's just a friend. I'm going out with Lissy tonight.'

'Oh yes, I forgot.' Claire's father chuckled. 'But you're a little overdressed for an evening at the Morton's.'

'He's going on a date, Dad.' Claire wanted the ground to swallow her up. 'Not with me.' She felt heat in her cheeks.

'Oh.'

Claire's mother opened her mouth to speak, and Claire decided that was definitely their cue to go. She ushered Adrian out of the room.

Adrian managed to squeak, 'thank you' as they left.

Her father shouted after them, 'You can keep the shoes, son. They never suited me anyway.' Though it was said in complete innocence, Claire cringed at the word 'son'.

A few minutes later, Adrian had collected his things and the pair stood in Claire's doorway.

'Um, sorry about that. I did tell them you were a friend. They must have forgotten...' Claire trailed off, sensing that the situation was growing more awkward as she babbled on.

'Don't worry about it.' Adrian tried to appear non-plussed, but Claire could tell by the way he ruffled his hair that he was nervous. 'I'll text you later. To let you know how it went.' He practically mouthed the last sentence, for fear of being overheard.

She nodded and watched him go, noting that his bum looked particularly pert as it made its way down the garden path. Claire couldn't actually take her eyes off it until he completely disappeared from view.

Lissy arrived twenty minutes later. A bubble of excited energy, she chattered away non-stop as soon as Claire sat in the passenger seat. They didn't have concrete plans for the evening, so when Claire casually suggested they try The Trout at High Tide, Lissy was all for it.

Once they'd arrived, however, Claire wasn't sure if it was such a good idea. Her intention had been to make sure Adrian was okay - anonymously, from a safe distance. His nerves had been almost palpable at Claire's house, and she'd wanted to protect him. But now they were actually there, she saw the reality of the situation: she was about to gate-crash her friend's first date - in a truly awkward, embarrassing manner, and with the added potential of being labelled a stalker. Claire felt butterflies in her stomach.

'Oh, I'm so excited! We haven't done anything like this in ages!' Lissy put her arm through Claire's. 'You've been overworking yourself lately, girl. It's that Dr Leach sucking the life out of you. I can't think of anything better than a nice meal out, just the two of us. The first glass of rosé is on me - just what the doctor ordered.' She winked. Lissy looked so happy, there was no way Claire could back out.

Walking into the restaurant was like stepping through the sound barrier. A hundred or so people, all talking at once. As they walked towards the 'wait here to be seated' sign, they had to weave round people gesturing expressively, their drinks in hand. Claire was nearly poked in the ear by one gentleman, who was so engrossed in his anecdote he didn't even notice.

The waiter told them there was a forty-five minute wait for a table. Lissy grabbed Claire's arm and dragged her to the bar. 'Sorry,' Claire mumbled.

Lissy waved her apology away. 'Don't sweat it. Just means there's more time for drinking.'

'Remember you're driving.'

'I know. But there are such things as mocktails.' Lissy tried to wave a barman down like she was hailing a taxi.

Claire scanned the room. There were so many people; every table was taken in the seating area and the bar was rammed full.

Adrian won't be able to spot me in this crowd. She relaxed a little but still found herself searching for him. Her heart fluttered whenever she saw a dark-haired guy, or a skinny guy, or a guy with glasses. She still hadn't found him when Lissy returned with their drinks.

'So, you remember Darrell, right? The guy I met at that bar a few weeks ago? Well, he's only told me he's a footballer! For a small team, mind, but still, a footballer...' Claire zoned out from Lissy's gossip; she looked over her shoulder and across the restaurant.

The place was dimly lit to encourage a certain ambience, but Claire eventually managed to spot Adrian's sparkling blue eyes from across the room. And, once she'd found him, she couldn't stop looking.

His table was practically in the centre of the room; it was meant for two people and, Claire had to admit, the pair appeared rather cosy. Claire's first impressions of 'Abiiii' had been spot on. She was petite, and wore a hot pink number that perfectly accentuated her figure. Her blonde hair fell in large, elegant curls, which bounced as she giggled. Adrian looked to be enjoying her company; Claire noted a number of excitable hand gestures and wide grins. Their eyes were locked together, and every now and again, one of them would touch the arms or the hands of the other – subtle signs of mutual affection, she conceded. Claire's face fell. Adrian didn't need any help.

'Hello? Earth to Claire-bear. You okay? Is the wine alright?' Claire looked back to find Lissy gazing at her with concern. Before she had chance to explain, the waiter showed them to their table.

Claire became struck with fear that they'd be seated next to Adrian; she held her breath as the waiter led them to a table three rows away from the couple. Though they weren't exactly sat on the knees of Adrian and his date, he only had to lift his eyes from Abi and briefly glance round the restaurant to spot them in plain view.

'Excuse me, are you sure this is our table?' Claire tried to keep her voice low so as not to attract any attention from the other diners (*particularly those three rows back!*), but it was difficult to be heard over the din of the restaurant. She had to repeat herself before the waiter replied.

'Why yes, miss.' The waiter seemed puzzled but kept a fake-but-professional smile on his lips. 'This is currently the only unoccupied table, and you ladies were next in line.' He pulled back a chair and nodded at Claire to sit down.

'But…we're sat right in the middle of the room. Everyone will be walking past us as we eat,' Claire protested.

The waiter didn't have chance to respond before Lissy sat in the chair he was offering. She took the menus from his hands. 'Don't worry, she's just being silly. This will be fine, thank you.' Lissy gave the waiter an apologetic smile then shot Claire a stern look that made her shut up and sit down. 'What's the matter with you?' Lissy hissed. 'The table's fine.'

'I'm just feeling a bit…claustrophobic.'

'You, claustrophobic? I told you working in that stuffy surgery's getting to you. Here.' Lissy passed Claire a menu. 'Relax. Enjoy.'

Claire did as she was told. The restaurant itself was lovely. The only thing bothering her was their proximity to Adrian - but how could she tell Lissy that? She stole a quick glance to her left; she needed have worried - Adrian and Abi were completely engrossed in one another and oblivious that Claire was there at all. She just had to get through the meal and leave with the same anonymity.

It'll be fine.

But after only a few minutes of furtive glancing between the food options and Adrian's table, panic got the better of her. She stood the menu on the table as a makeshift screen and ducked behind it, her nose almost touching the page. Lissy stared blankly at the embossed leather folder in front of her, in place of the friend she'd sat down with. She picked up Claire's glass of wine and sniffed it, before reaching over and lowering the menu. 'Everything okay?'

'Um, yeah, definitely. I just don't know what to have! It all sounds so yummy.' Claire opted for the first thing she recognised when the waiter returned to take their orders. There was a brief tug-of-war as he tried to collect Claire's menu, which he won. He sauntered off, leaving her exposed.

'Claire, what is going on? You're acting so strange. Are you ill?' All Lissy got in response was an unintelligible mumble. She watched Claire shield her face with her hand and was just about to stop a waiter to ask for help when suddenly her oversized scarlet handbag was heaved onto the table. 'Claire! What the hell...?'

'Oh, Lissy, this handbag is gorgeous! Where's it from?' Claire knew that no matter how many questions Lissy had, she wouldn't be able to resist a conversation about handbags.

'I was hoping you'd notice! I only got it this week, from

that new place that's opened in the village - next to the newsagents, opposite the bakery. I was a bit put off at first. I mean a bag shop, in Dovedon? Seriously? But I'm so glad I went in there. It's like vintage meets chic, but in a good way...'

Claire had zoned out of the conversation again; despite her best efforts, she couldn't stop glancing at Adrian's table from behind Lissy's bright-red handbag.

When the food arrived, she had to admit, it looked and smelled divine. The plates were modern and square, and framed the food perfectly, and the sauce had been drizzled, not poured. Had it been any other occasion, Claire would have thoroughly enjoyed her evening, and taken the time to appreciate everything going on around her. Tonight, however, she couldn't settle. She practically inhaled her food, not wanting to stay one minute longer than necessary.

As the evening progressed, she couldn't help feeling like an intruder. All she wanted was to leave quietly and let Adrian continue his first date in peace. She felt relieved when Lissy didn't order dessert - as soon as they'd paid, they could be out of there. She'd done it. She'd managed to avoid being spotted by Adrian and his date, and enjoyed a nice meal out with her friend at the same time.

Whilst waiting for the bill, the couple at the adjacent table ordered a 'Sizzling Fajita'. The Trout at High Tide was famous for the dish, and the waiters made a big deal when bringing it to diners' tables. They added extra-hot spices to create a billowing cloud of smoke as it was served.

But when the waiter passed, the spicy smoke made Claire's eyes smart. Even worse, Lissy had taken a deep breath just as the fajita appeared, which left her coughing and gasping for air. Claire felt the people around them look over with concern. Lissy grabbed hold of her handbag, frantically rifling through it for something to help bring her coughing fit to a halt.

Completely exposed, Claire panicked.   She was about to

crawl under the table when a member of staff came over to offer Lissy assistance.

Claire leaned forward so that the waiter was in Adrian's eye line. Lissy gulped down the large glass of water offered and the madness began to calm.

Claire waited for the right moment to glance over the waiter's shoulder, to determine whether the fajita commotion had caught Adrian's attention. To her horror, she saw that the pair had vanished.

Her eyes raced around the room;. She prayed that Adrian and Abi weren't making their way over to help the woman who had, by the sounds of it, coughed up a lung. When she looked towards the door, she caught sight of Adrian holding it open for the little blonde. She saw Abi cling tightly to Adrian's blazer draped around her shoulders, and as they departed, the last thing Claire noted was the huge smile on Adrian's face.

'I'm fine, babe, thanks for asking,' said Lissy. She rustled around in her handbag and found her compact mirror, then spent a few moments dabbing at her eye makeup with a napkin.

Claire knew she'd been a terrible friend that night, on more than one level. She could have potentially ruined one friend's first date, and she'd also left her best friend to suffer a horrendous coughing attack alone.

Lissy snapped the compact shut, leant across the table and took Claire's limp hand. 'Okay, spill. You've been acting strange all night. I thought you were going to let me choke to death just then. What on earth is going on?'

Claire straightened herself up. There was no point lying - Lissy would see straight through any story, bleary-eyed or not.

'Sorry, I shouldn't have...' Claire began, but Lissy waved away her apology for the second time that evening. *Typical Lissy, always wants to get straight to the gossip.* 'My friend Adrian was here tonight, on a date.'

'Adrian? The guy you met at the bookstore?' Lissy seemed confused, but intrigued.

Claire hadn't told Lissy much about him; she wasn't sure why, as she usually told her best friend everything. But when it came to Adrian, Claire had stopped herself - like he was a secret, and if she'd told Lissy the full details, she risked him disappearing from her life as quickly as he'd arrived.

After splitting from Muscles, and the miserable weeks that followed, Claire had felt her world turn grey. Adrian brought a rainbow with him, and she was scared that if she told anyone, the magic would be broken.

She'd just seen her ray of sunshine walk out the door with another woman. It was confession time.

Claire told Lissy that she'd met up with Adrian numerous times since their first meeting, and that they'd hit it off. She described her visit to Oddballs, and also told her about the setting up of their online dating profiles - and how she'd helped him pick a shirt for his date that evening.

When she happened to mention that the shirt she'd chosen was the same shade as Adrian's eyes, her friend's face changed. 'You've got the hots for him!' Lissy's eyes twinkled. 'Don't deny it.'

'No, I haven't,' Claire said quickly. 'He's just a friend. A really good friend.'

Lissy shook her head, a huge grin on her face. 'A friend whose eyes you know so well you can pick out the same colour shirt? Come on, Claire, admit it. You've got the butterflies.'

At that moment, Claire's stomach wasn't full of butterflies; all she could feel was her scampi churning. Her mind was in overdrive. 'Why would two people on a first date leave a restaurant this early?' she asked.

Lissy raised an eyebrow. 'You really want me to answer that?' Claire felt herself blush. 'That isn't the question you should be asking. The real question is what are we going to do to put you back on top?' Claire could see her predicament was giving Lissy ideas. The woman was now on a mission.

If Claire did have feelings for Adrian, she hadn't realised it. She'd suggested the dating site with complete innocence, but now feared her plan had backfired.

Whether it was the wine talking, she didn't know. *Am I jealous of Abi on a romantic level, or do I just resent the thought she might steal my 'platonic' friend away?*

She tuned into Lissy's plans, which were already taking shape. Either way, it sounded like Claire would soon get her answer.

Chapter Nine

"Communication lies at the heart of many problems. If in doubt, speak out"

Outside Oddballs the following Tuesday, Lissy made everything seem simple.

'Don't worry, it'll be fine. I'll natter to the sweet old ladies, you knit a few rows and shoot meaningful looks in Adrian's direction while tossing your hair.' Lissy nudged Claire's arm playfully. 'Maybe even throw him a sultry pout or two.' She puckered her lips. 'He'll soon realise what he's missing. You guys can carry on where you left off, and I'll be home in time for the soaps. Mission accomplished.' Before Claire could even think of protesting, Lissy had marched them both into the shop.

Claire wasn't too worried; she trusted her friend completely. Over the years, she'd stood in the wings and watched whilst Lissy effortlessly moved from relationship to relationship; winning over men, winning them back, changing their minds, and even batting some of them away. Lissy was smart, beautiful and funny, what was there not to love? So, when it came to men, if Lissy told Claire to jump, she would happily ask, 'How high?'

Once inside Oddballs introductions were made. Adrian reached out to shake Lissy's hand. *A little formal…?* Claire was shocked to see Lissy sport a goofy grin in response.

'Erm, can we join the Stitch and Bitch this afternoon?' Claire interrupted.

'Of course,' he replied. He seemed over the moon at the suggestion.

She smiled nervously and dragged Lissy to his office for a couple of extra chairs. 'What was all that about?' Claire hissed.

'What?' Lissy whispered back.

'The crazy lady grin you gave Adrian back there?'

Lissy giggled. 'Sorry. You know what I'm like at keeping secrets. I thought it was better than blurting out something I'd regret.'

Claire was familiar with Lissy's motor-mouth. She was particularly terrible around Christmas. 'Okay, I'll let you off. But tone down the crazy stare.'

Lissy crossed her eyes, which made Claire laugh and relax a little. *Wow, when did I get so tense?*

Now that they were actually there, sat around the large wooden table, knitting in hand, it seemed like the worst idea the pair had ever had. Adrian was only an arm's length away. He was not just in eye-shot, but earshot, too. He'd hear every word spoken, and he'd also see every woolly failure Claire would inevitably make.

Claire's fingers fumbled over the tiny red loops on her needle. She counted each one, over and over again. Next to her, Lissy scrutinised a ball of Barbie-pink wool like it was an ancient artefact. 'I thought you'd like that colour,' said Claire, wondering if she'd made the wrong choice. After all, she wanted her friend to enjoy herself, regardless of their ulterior motive.

'Oh, yeah, I do.' Lissy looked at Claire sheepishly. 'I just don't know where to start.'

In just a few moments Claire had delved into the centre of Lissy's ball of wool and spilled its guts across the table. She had begun to wind the wool when the bell above Oddballs' door trilled. The Bitches had arrived. Claire and Lissy exchanged a look.

Here's goes nothing… Claire glanced at Adrian, but he was busy writing something on a clipboard.

'Claire, dearie, it's lovely to see you again.' Rene came to the table first. 'Come to give it another try?' Rene pointed at the explosion of wool strewn across the table, a genuine smile on her lips.

'Something like that.' Claire stumbled over her words. Embarrassed about the mess she'd made, she scooped up what she could of Lissy's wool, and dumped it in her friend's lap.

'And who's this you've brought along today?' The crow's feet at the corner of Rene's eyes deepened with her smile.

'This is Lis...er, Melissa. My oldest and dearest friend.'

Lissy scowled at her friend when she heard her full name, then turned her attention to Rene and gave her a sweet smile. Claire knew how much Lissy hated her real name, but she saw these ladies as respectable, older women who enjoyed knitting, fine dining, sweet tea, and completing the crossword on a Sunday afternoon. 'Lissy' just didn't feel appropriate, somehow.

The other ladies settled into their chairs; greetings were given and further introductions made. 'Is that what I think it is?' Gladys pointed at the few short rows in Claire's hands.

She swallowed. 'Um, it's a start.'

'Give it here then, let's have a look.' Claire sat in horror as her needles and wool were passed round the circle. *They're scrutinising every split stitch, every tension change, every mistake!*

Her work made it back to Gladys. She brought Claire's knitting millimetres from her face and squinted at it. Claire held her breath.

'Whatever were you on about the other week? This knitting's fine! You've got nothing to worry about.' Gladys passed the knitting back.

Claire looked at the four straggly rows with fresh eyes - without influence from her past knitting conquests and with no preconceptions. She saw them as they were: four rows of garter stitch.

Maybe it isn't that bad. She continued to wind Lissy's wool before seizing her own needles with more confidence than she'd had for weeks.

Everyone focused on their wool and needles.

'So, Rene, how did Jenny's scan go?'

'Oh, it was beautiful. I finally got to see my great-grand-child!' Rene's eyes glistened. A chorus of coos rose from the table.

Doreen gently tapped Lissy's arm and whispered, 'Jenny is Rene's granddaughter. She's chosen Rene as her birthing partner. It's so sweet. After everything she went through with Charlie last year - that was Rene's late husband, dear - this is doing her the world of good.'

Claire looked at Rene's needles. They were shaping a petite lemon square. On the table sat a finished square of similar size, in mint green. Claire picked it up and held it between her thumb and forefinger. She couldn't believe its softness. 'Are you knitting this for the baby, Rene?'

'Yes, love, I'm knitting a blanket. I'm going to do squares in different stitches, so the baby will have lots of things to feel. It's a great way to learn some new techniques; I'm still a learner here, really. I should be wearing my L-plates.' Rene chuckled, a sound that warmed Claire's heart.

'L-plates!' scoffed Gladys. 'We've promised her that, by June, she'll have a blanket and a whole outfit to match.'

'Now, now girls, let's not run away with ourselves,' Rene giggled.

'Mint and lemon,' said Claire, smiling - it was infectious. 'When will you know the gender of the baby?'

'We're leaving it a surprise. It's Jenny's first child, so we're trying to do everything properly.' Claire noted how much the subject lit up Rene's face. She wanted to scoop the old lady up and cuddle her.

As they knitted, the table became a woolly rainbow: thick yarns and thin yarns, big balls and small skeins, in an array of colours. They were each creating something completely different and Claire couldn't help being inquisitive. *What the hell...my knitting has already done the rounds.*

Gladys's project caught her eye next, or more so, the gigantic ball of grey wool that blocked her from view. 'That's a big ball of wool, Gladys,' Claire joked, leaning around it for comic effect.

'This is just one of many! I've got another six of these at home.'

Claire's eyes widened. 'What are you making?'

Gladys's hands and needles emerged above the huge ball of wool. They looked to be creating a tank top, and every row was perfectly neat. Claire was sad to see it disappear again behind the aran. 'I've only got seven months until the next school year starts, and this year the youngest one moves up to big school. We'll have at least one in every year then, so I thought I best get knitting now. Can't have my grandkids getting cold - they need their school jumpers in the winter! Big families need big balls of wool,' she said proudly. 'Just seeing them all lined up in my jumpers on the first day back makes it all worthwhile.'

'She does it every year,' added Beryl. 'She's so quick. I wish I could knit at half the speed she does.'

'Oh, stop it, Beryl, you'll make me blush!' Gladys half-protested, beaming at the compliment.

'No, I mean it! Look.' Beryl lifted her own needles and held them next to Gladys's. Beryl's multi-coloured tube looked tiny in comparison to Gladys's tank top. 'My chicken jumpers aren't even half the size of your school jumpers, and we started them at the same time.'

'Eh? Chicken jumpers? I thought they had feathers,' piped up Lissy, perplexed.

'I wished they all did, dear,' said Beryl. 'I'm knitting these for the local hen rescue. They help ex-battery hens stay warm, which encourages the regrowth of their feathers. Poor little things. It's a wonderful charity, and the pattern's so simple. You'll have to give it a go sometime. I'm sure a little hen somewhere would be very grateful of your jumper.'

Lissy looked at her ball of pink wool thoughtfully. 'Maybe I will,' she mused. Although chickens were not the cuddliest of animals, Claire knew that Lissy would be determined to knit them a jumper one day after hearing that story.

Next to Lissy was Doreen, silently knitting from a slender skein of wool, which was elegantly twisted into a fine but luxurious braid. Following the yarn from the skein to the needles, Claire found it was attached to the most delicate-looking lacework she'd ever laid eyes on. It put the many books Claire had seen on the subject to shame.

'What are you knitting, Doreen? That looks fiddly,' asked Lissy, also mesmerised by the lacework.

'My husband and I are hoping to book a cruise for the autumn, so I'm making a few shawls in case it gets a bit nippy from the sea breeze.'

'A cruise! That sounds wonderful,' Lissy sighed.

'She makes toys, too,' Beryl chipped in again. 'You'll have to bring them some pictures next time, Doreen. They're so intricate. Little works of art.' The others nodded enthusiastically.

'Oh, please! I'd love to see them,' said Claire.

Doreen laughed politely. 'I'll try and remember to bring some, then. So, we'll definitely see you next time?' She looked at both Lissy and Claire with a smile.

'I don't see why not,' Claire replied happily. She glanced at Lissy who had yet to take her eyes off Doreen's shawl; she was nodding in agreement. 'Meeting all of you and seeing your projects is quite inspirational. I feel like I've got my confidence back...and I haven't even touched a stitch yet!'

Everyone laughed warmly and Claire felt at peace. *Why have I never thought about a knitting group before?* A support group should have been her first port of call when her knitting started to (literally) fall apart. One of the many reasons, she conceded, why meeting Adrian had been a blessing.

'And what about you, Lissy?' said Doreen. 'How do you feel about your knitting?'

Lissy looked sheepish. 'I've never picked up a ball of wool or needles in my life,' she admitted. 'I think I could try and have a go at the knitting bit…nothing fancy, mind. But I can't figure out how you get the stitches on the needle in the first place.'

Doreen smiled. 'Pass it here, dear, I'll cast on for you.' She gently placed her own knitting on the table and reached for Lissy's needles and wool. 'What shall we begin with, then? A scarf or a blanket?'

Claire had become so carried away with her knitting, and with Lissy's first attempts, and discovering more about the ladies' projects, that it wasn't until halfway through the session that she remembered the real reason she and Lissy had come. As soon as there was a lull in conversation, when everyone was concentrating hard on their individual projects – Rene's tongue sticking out from between her lips as she focused - Claire snuck a look at Adrian.

He was stood to the left of the knitting table. Clutching his clipboard, he searched through the various shelves, making notes as he did so and intermittently chewing the end of his pen. Claire was within his peripheral vision at best. There was no hope of making eye contact from where she sat.

As everyone at the table had their heads down, any attempts at flirting would at least pass the ladies by, she reckoned. In one movement, Claire flicked her hair over her left shoulder, her auburn curls cascading down her back. The light caught it, which highlighted the copper and red tones. She once again snatched a glance at Adrian, and was disappointed that he hadn't even turned round. Claire tutted quietly.

One more go…

She moved her hand up to the nape of her neck and used it to send her curls soaring; as she did this, she swished her head from side to side to make the most of the movement.

Adrian was still oblivious.

Once more.

Still no response.

Last time…

For this attempt, Claire turned her whole neck from left to right; her curls flung round with such ferocity, they nearly found themselves in Lissy's mouth.

'Are you okay, love? Slept funny?' Claire found Rene staring at her, concern on her face.

'Oh, no, no. Just, um, my hair…tickling my neck. Nothing to worry about.'

'Maybe you'd benefit from tying your hair up while you knit? I'd offer you a bobble, but I haven't used those in years.' Rene patted her neat bob fondly. She returned her attention to her squares.

Lissy, initially confused by the explosion of hair in her face, appeared to cotton on to what Claire was attempting. She swivelled in her chair to look across at Adrian, but he was still engrossed with his clipboard. She looked at Claire and gave a sulky pout.

Claire shrugged. 'I give up,' she mouthed.

'Do it again,' Lissy mouthed back, before erupting into a coughing fit.

'Oh, love! You okay?' Doreen started to rub Lissy's back and the other ladies put down their knitting. Lissy caught everyone's attention but Adrian's, who instead squinted intently at a particular ball of wool.

'I think that's our cue to make the drinks. What's everyone having?' Beryl picked up her pad and pen.

'We'll go,' Claire said quickly, already out of her seat and grabbing Lissy's hand. 'We'll be back in a tick.'

For the rest of the Stitch and Bitch, Claire kept her head down. Going at a snail's pace, she'd reached the end of one row by the time the ladies were ready to pack up. Her passion, confidence and enthusiasm had fizzled out. Glumly, she packed away her things, speaking for Lissy when offering to wash up. She was desperate to creep away before everyone said their goodbyes.

Upstairs, Lissy was adamant. 'You can't give up now.' She'd have crossed her arms if they weren't submerged in water.

'Yes, I can. You can tell it's bad. I even considered the sultry pout.' Claire pulled her best duck face and Lissy giggled.

'It could be worse. I really don't think he's ignoring you - he just chose a stupid day to do a stock-take!'

They headed back downstairs after the washing up was done. Claire remained hopeful that she could catch Adrian's attention as they departed. As she reached the bottom step she saw that he'd stopped counting his stock and was now serving a customer.

'That was a nice young lady friend I saw you with the other night, Ade. I was walking past your house just as you were showing her in.' The guy winked and nudged Adrian's arm. In Claire's opinion, he wasn't the typical Oddballs' customer; he was tall, muscular, and covered in tattoos (and not of the knitting variety). *Very 'laddish' in nature.*

'Sorry, Darren, I never saw you.'

'Don't worry, mate. You were understandably distracted.' Darren winked again. 'Anyway, best get these back home to Mum or I'll be in big trouble. Catch you later.' Claire watched Darren stride out of the shop.

Claire was about to approach Adrian, a sweet smile in place and neck geared up for some more hair-flicking, when she thought about what Darren had said.

He took Abi home?

Claire hadn't realised she'd zoned out until she was jolted back to reality by Lissy's elbow jabbing at her side. Her eyes focused, and she found Adrian smiling at her expectantly. 'Sorry?' Claire's voice was distant.

'Your afternoon. How was it?'

'Oh, fine. But we better get going. Bye.' Claire scooped up her bag and made for the door, expecting Lissy to follow.

'Will I see you next week?' Adrian called after them, but his words were lost as the bell over the door clamoured from the force Claire had applied in her desperation to leave.

'What was all that about?' Lissy asked breathlessly, when she finally caught up with Claire.

'Nothing. Let's just go home.'

'I thought we were going for a spectacular ending.' Lissy sounded either confused or upset - or both. Claire didn't want to look across at her friend's face to find out which.

'Just take me home, please,' she said quietly. She could feel the prickle of tears in the corner of her eyes. Lissy had known Claire long enough to know that now was not the time to push. She backed off and did as Claire asked.

Claire flopped onto her bed after throwing her knitting bag across the room. As it landed, red wool spilled out as the ball rolled across the floor. But Claire wasn't looking. She stared blankly at the ceiling. She'd achieved nothing. It wasn't as if she'd expected anything to actually happen, but the whole afternoon had been a disaster where Adrian was concerned. The only conclusion she'd come to was that he was very happy with Abi.

She delved into her handbag for her mobile phone. Laying back, she pressed an icon on the Home screen that bore a picture of a small fish. The app began to load; as it did so, her stomach churned. She predicted she'd find 'no matches', and that she'd spend the rest of the evening gazing at Adrian's profile. So she was shocked to see a speech bubble waiting for her.

Hello :)

She stared at the phone for a moment whilst processing the message. Admittedly, the greeting was short, but the smiley-face made it sweet. It was an invitation to converse, an acknowledgement that she existed, and a compliment, all rolled into one.

This is how it starts! All she had to do was respond, but her fingers hesitated over the on-screen keyboard.

Adrian was sent the exact same greeting from Abi, and he didn't hesitate, did he?

She stared at the message for a few moments longer. Eventually, she sat up and began to type.

Chapter Ten

"Never substitute what you truly desire"

Claire had never been fashionably late to a date before, but if this bus didn't hurry up, she would be. Shivering at the bus stop, she knew that her floral floaty dress and cream stilettos had been a mistake. It was further evidence that she was out of the dating loop; she'd not had a clue what she should wear and, in the end, opted for pretty over practical. All she could do was pray that her date wasn't expecting her to join him in a half-marathon, or his plans for their afternoon didn't include rock climbing.

As Claire envisioned such horrors, the bus rounded the corner. She got on hurriedly, just happy to escape the cruel wind. She took her usual seat: bottom left, second from the back, and she'd just managed to retrieve her MP3 player from the bottom of her handbag when, out of corner of her eye, she saw a man get out of his seat and move towards the vacant one beside her. Not keen on the idea of a conversation with a total stranger, Claire hastily reached for her earphones, but before she had to chance to get them in her ears the man sat next to her.

'Claire?'

She turned sharply, confused why he should recognise her. It took a few moments, but she eventually realised that Dan, her mysterious date, was also riding the number fifty-seven bus.

'Well, fancy seeing you here!' He turned awkwardly in his seat and pulled Claire into a hug. He wore a well-loved, black leather jacket, which stuck to Claire's cheek as they embraced. 'It's great to finally meet you.' Dan released her and leaned back in his seat. 'And we already have something in common!' He gestured to the bus they were riding, a grin across his face. Claire laughed, but inside she felt herself cringing from head to toe. *What am I supposed to say to that?*

Luckily, Dan was more than happy to chat without needing much response. He told Claire all about his mum and dad, the house he shared with them, and his part-time job. Claire nodded appropriately, noting that they actually did have a fair amount in common. By the time they reached Dovedon, Claire had changed her first impression, and was actually starting to warm to Dan and his sticky leather jacket.

'So, where are we going?' asked Claire, as Dan led them into the centre of the village. *Maybe we're going to get a connecting service…the bus to the train station is quite frequent. The world's our oyster! Shopping, the cinema…a beach-side retreat..!*

'Into Dovedon.' Dan's grin hadn't moved since he'd sat next to her on the bus. 'I want to introduce you to some of my local hideouts.'

Claire groaned inwardly. She could guarantee there wasn't a single place in Dovedon she hadn't seen before, and she could honestly say there wasn't a single place she wanted to see, either. She'd thought her worst nightmare would have involved running a marathon during their date; visiting Dovedon was a close second. As they walked up familiar streets Claire reviewed the situation. Dovedon, although boring and designed for the retired, wasn't far from home. Although she'd learned rather a lot about Dan already, they were still little more than strangers. She was out, on her own, with a guy she hardly knew; at least there was no hope of her getting lost or led astray. Dovedon was within her comfort zone. If the date went horribly wrong, she could jump on a bus back home or phone for a taxi. If she had to, she could even walk home.

Dovedon, during early afternoon, had to be the safest date ever. *Maybe that's exactly why he planned this. It's kind of sweet when you think about it - he must be a true gent…*

Their first stop was Cee-Dees, the town's one and only music shop. Dan grabbed hold of Claire's hand as soon as they walked through the door. He guided her past the vinyls and the easy listening, and headed straight to the rock and heavy metal section. His hand was warm, maybe a little sweaty, but his grip was firm and comforting. Just as Claire began to enjoy the feeling, Dan let go and began rapidly flicking through the CDs.

He plucked a case from the shelf and held it inches from Claire's nose. 'Have you ever listened to "The Dingbatz"?' She stared at the CD. The cover depicted a bat hanging upside down with its wings spread as it clung onto a piece of barbed wire. The tiny mammal had its mouth open wide, showing off a set of sharp-looking fangs. She shook her head. Claire had never heard of 'The Dingbatz'.

'You should, they're *a-maz-ing!* I saw them last year at MetalFest. They were brilliant! Tore it up, they did. My ears were ringing for days afterwards!' Dan laughed and shook his head as he relived the memory. Claire gave a thin smile, not entirely sure if having your ears ringing for days was a good thing. But it was clear Dan loved that band. *Well, if someone's willing to risk their own hearing for them, they must be good.*

Dan popped the CD back in the rack and continued to flick through the rest. Soon, his fingers stopped again; this time, he pulled out a case that had an acid-green cover, which made Claire's eyes sting. 'What about "The Punkstranauts"?'

She shook her head again. 'Sorry.'

'No need to apologise, babe. It just means you've got a lot of good music to catch up on. Let me start with the basics.' With that Dan put 'The Punkstranauts' back to search the CDs again.

Babe? Claire let his endearment sink in. *Is he being sweet? Is he coming on to me, or has he just forgotten my name?* She couldn't decide. She decided to let it lie, and watched as he foraged through the section.

At first, Claire enjoyed herself. Dan was opening her eyes

to a completely new genre of music. The excitement and passion in his voice made it difficult to resist. At one point, Claire was utterly convinced she needed 'The Death Mental Pirates', and their song 'Take Me to Gallows', in her life. She'd almost snatched the CD out of Dan's hand.

By the time the hundredth CD was thrust in her face, the excitement began to fade and Claire's attention span wore thin. When Dan seemed particularly engrossed in his search, Claire took the opportunity to wander off. She mooched aimlessly down the rest of the aisles, wondering why, despite row upon row of CDs, she hadn't heard of any band or artist.

At the end of the third aisle, Claire took her mobile from her bag and, in the notes' section, wrote: 'Listen to more music'. She clicked 'save'. *God I feel old. Surely I'm not that out of touch?* Then she remembered the last time she'd ventured into town for a night out with Lissy. Neither of them had recognised a single song coming from the club's fancy speakers. After just an hour of music that made their heads pound, they'd took refuge in the cheesy 'Nineties Bar' across the street. Claire sighed. *Old doesn't even begin to cover it.*

Moving into the next aisle, she was reunited with Dan. Claire waited for a reprimand of some sort for wandering off, but his grin didn't falter. 'Ready for our next stop?'

'Yes.' Claire breathed a sigh of relief. *Maybe there I won't feel like a golden oldie.*

They left Cee-Dees and headed up the high street. Then Dan stopped at the door to the indoor market. 'Ladies first,' he said, holding it open for her.

Dovedon Market was a traditional mismatch of stalls. From ladies' lingerie to bric-a-brac, from homemade cakes to second-hand games, if you couldn't find what you were looking for on the high street, you would find it in the market. But Claire couldn't work out why Dan had taken her there. They passed the homeware store and the butchers, the sportswear stall and the bakery. He didn't even look twice at the games stand or the sweet shop. Claire frowned. *What could he possibly want in here?*

She wasn't left wondering for long. Tucked away at the back of the market, the furthest stall to the left, was a shop Claire had never seen before. Over the entrance was a sign that said 'Strings and Picks'. As they got closer, Claire noticed a line of brightly-coloured guitars of all shapes and sizes, hung across the back wall. Dan headed straight for them.

'Dan, my man!' An old rocker-type emerged from behind a huge amp.

'Gazza!' The two men performed a series of mutual slaps, fist-bumps and handshakes, before sharing a man hug.

Gazza wore an oversized t-shirt promoting a group Claire didn't recognise. *No surprise there.* He had long, blonde hair and - unnecessarily so, in Claire's opinion - wore sunglasses. Indoors.

'And who's this?' Gazza nodded in Claire's direction, lowering his glasses to get a better look.

'This is my friend Claire,' Dan said hurriedly, like an over-excited puppy.

'Well, any friend of Dan's is a friend of mine. Welcome!' Gazza offered up his hand for a high five. Gingerly, Claire slapped his palm, hoping that it wouldn't evolve into anything more. 'Do you play?' Gazza gestured to the wall of guitars.

'Um, no.' Claire shook her head, suddenly feeling out of place in a guitar shop when she'd never held one in her life.

'Aw, Dan. Looks like it's your time to shine!' Gazza disappeared again behind the amp. When he returned, he held a flame-coloured guitar. 'Show her how it's done, man.' He held out the guitar to Dan, who snatched it up, slung the strap over his head, and raised his arm, poised.

'I was hoping you'd say that.' He winked at Claire.

Waaaaaaaaaaaaammm! The guitar strings shuddered into life at Dan's fingertips. He raised his hand in the air, devil horns up, before clearing his throat. There was a second of pure silence before he struck the strings again. Then he began singing at the top of his voice.

It made a change that Claire knew the song. She knew it well. Her dad often spoke of Bon Jovi in a whimsical way, and their albums were the soundtrack of all long drives.

'We've gotta hold on to what we've got. It doesn't make a difference if we make or not!'

People stopped going about their business, and now stared into the guitar stall with bemused looks on their faces. Dan was blissfully unaware of the attention he'd attracted, his eyes shut. He was immersed in his jamming session. 'We've got each other and that's a lot. For love, we'll give it a shot!'

Claire stared in horror at the small crowd forming. Some bobbed their heads to the noise from Dan's guitar, others stifled laughter behind their hands. Claire felt her cheeks flush. *Surely this can't get any worse...* She wanted the ground to swallow her up.

'Wooooah! We're halfway there. Wooooah-oh! Living on a Claire!' Dan shrieked, dropping to his knees in front of her. Claire was stunned. *Oh, it just did.*

The crowd let out a burst of laughter, which jolted Dan from his performance. Suddenly shy, he straightened up and removed the guitar, shoving it towards Gazza, who was in hysterics. The show over, the crowd began to drift away. Claire was glued to the spot, her face the colour of a tomato.

'D-did you like that?' Dan stammered. Claire just glared.

'Looks like your plan fell flat, kiddo.' Gazza was trying to mask the fact he was still laughing. 'You owe me a fiver.'

'A fiver? For what?' Claire said, puzzled.

'Hey! I can't set up something like this for nothing! A man's got to eat.'

Claire couldn't quite believe what she was hearing. It was bad enough that she'd been subjected to such an experience, but to be mortified intentionally – well, that was a different story. 'That was planned?!'

'I thought you might like it,' mumbled Dan. 'Girls dig a guy with an instrument, right?'

'I'm not listening to this.' Claire held up her hand, hoping to terminate the conversation.

'You said online that you like surprises!' Dan's voice raised a few octaves. Claire didn't respond; instead, she stormed off towards the exit.

She was grateful for the cool wind as she stepped outside. As her embarrassment subsided, she felt a dull ache radiating from her feet. An afternoon of walking in stiletto heels hadn't done her feet any favours, and now she was paying the price. She could just imagine the size of the blister on her left heel.

Dan caught up with Claire, but neither of them spoke. They just walked aimlessly down the street.

Eventually, he broke the silence. 'I'm starving.' *Finally.* Claire felt relief wash over her. *A nice sit-down meal. The chance for Dan to redeem himself. The chance to talk, properly.* Although Dovedon was quite dull, she knew of a few nice restaurants on the outskirts of town.

'Fancy a bag of chips? My treat.' Dan grinned at Claire expectantly, as if he'd just offered her dinner at The Ritz. Claire just looked at him. Yes, she was hungry, but a bag of chips was not the sort of meal she'd had in mind.

Fifteen minutes later, they made their way back to the bus stop, chips in hand. Claire couldn't wait to get home. Dan rambled on about a band he'd seen the week before, and how 'sick' the 'mosh' had been. She hobbled along beside him, silently praying that the bus would arrive soon.

As they reached the stop, Dan sucked his thumb and first finger noisily. Then he dumped the greasy bag of chips in her arms. 'There you go, babe, you can have them for the journey.' He smiled at her before bounding across the road.

Claire, utterly bemused, called after him, 'I thought we were getting the same bus?'

'This one's quicker for me,' he hollered, as a double-decker breached the end of the road. 'See ya!' He waved from the window as it pulled away. Claire looked down at the greasy bag of chips and grimaced. If anyone should have had a quick escape from their date, it should have been her.

She decided that Dan was most certainly not her 'fish'. She vowed to delete the infernal app, and every single memory that went with it.

When Claire logged on to FishTank, however, with every intention of deleting her profile, she was surprised to find a message in her inbox. She feared it was from Dan, proposing a second date, but instead, there was a new face - Ben - smiling up at her from the screen. *Not again.* Her curiosity got the better of her; soon, Claire and Ben were virtually acquainted.

A week later, Claire was on a train, feeling giddy about Ben's invitation to brunch. Brunch was different, quirky, against the norm. It made Ben sound like a rule breaker, and Claire liked that. Plus, there was mystery – would she have breakfast, or lunch?

Ben had suggested a place called Angels, which she hoped would prove a heavenly experience. She met him at the train station, and he initially appeared to be everything a girl could want: tall, dark and handsome. He took Claire's arm in his, a gesture that had her swooning just a little, and led the way. But as they left the train station via the rear entrance, and started down a narrow side street, Claire became a little alarmed. *Maybe it's just a shortcut? A scary, kind of grotty, shortcut...*

When Ben stopped outside a poky, greasy spoon of a café, Claire's heart sank. Angels turned out to be 'Ange L's'. His favourite 'restaurant' was a cheap diner, though it appeared the perfect place for people who fancied breakfast for lunch.

For Claire, though, brunch no longer seemed mysterious…or appetising.

As they entered, Claire's senses were hit with an overpowering smell of grease mixed with egg. She just knew, by the way it hung in the air, that her hair would smell of the place for days. For a fleeting moment Claire considered running away, but when she looked at Ben, with his perfect white smile and chiselled jawline, pulling back one of the red plastic chairs for her to sit down, her heart melted. She had to stay, just in case.

When the food arrived, it swam in its own juices. Even Claire's simple egg on toast had a grey tinge. She picked at her food and eventually gave up.

'So, how long have you been online dating?' he asked. Claire watched as little bits of hash brown erupted from his mouth onto the table.

'A few weeks,' she replied, covertly adjusting the tablecloth so that the crumbs didn't fall in her lap. 'You?'

'A few months.' Ben smiled proudly, like it was some kind of achievement. Claire could see bits of food stuck in his teeth. 'I've been on loads of dates, just not found anyone suitable.' He continued to talk with his mouth full, spraying food everywhere. Claire was glad she'd finished, and that the welfare of her plate was not her problem.

On first sight, Claire had liked Ben's casual look - a red checked shirt, left open over a white vest. But the baked beans *had* been rather runny, and walking round with a man sporting orange sauce down his front was not attractive in the slightest. By the end of the day, Claire learnt not to judge a book by its cover (unless that cover was Ange L's); although Ben was beautiful, he wasn't house trained. And so, when Ben went in for a kiss, Claire offered her cheek, and the pair agreed to go their separate ways.

On the basis that her dates had been ordeals rather than romantic experiences, Claire abandoned FishTank. She didn't dare touch the app after her adventures with Dan the Man and Bean Sauce Ben. But after a glass of wine too many, during a girly night at Lissy's, things got out of hand.

'Oh, please, Claire. Come on, it'll be fun!' All night, Lissy had pestered Claire to look for young, sexy singles in her area. 'What if I know somebody on there? That would be sooo funny.'

Claire rolled her eyes. 'Lissy, it's not a game. These are real people.'

'I know.' Lissy gave an exaggerated nod. 'But maybe we'll find someone who's ferociously handsome?' She raised her eyebrows suggestively and they burst into giggles.

'Okay,' Claire caved. 'Five minutes. But I'm holding the phone.'

Half an hour later, Claire was still holding the phone and Lissy was still scrolling through faces, occasionally giving shrieks of delight or grunts of distaste.

'Lissy, I've really got to pee.' Claire had started to wriggle around on the sofa.

'Go, then. I've got this.' Lissy's tongue poked out as she concentrated, her eyes fixed on the screen.

Claire hadn't intended to leave Lissy unattended with the app. But she'd behaved herself for half-an-hour, and Claire really needed to pee. She could trust her best friend, just this once.

She'd been in the bathroom five seconds when she heard, 'Whoopsie!'

'Lissy! What have you done?' Claire raced back into the room.

'What does it mean when you click the eye icon?'

'It means I've winked at someone!' Claire grabbed her phone from Lissy, who began to giggle hysterically.

Lissy had 'winked' at a trendy looking bearded man. In his profile picture, he wore an ice blue suit with a crisp white shirt. His jet black hair was slicked back perfectly.

From what Claire could tell, his page was that of a sea-soned online dater. His profile was sleek and streamlined.

He was a guy who knew what he wanted and wasn't afraid to take his time. *A guy like that will get a lot of attention on an app like this. It was a mistake, after all. A wink doesn't actually mean anything.*

Confident that her wink would be lost in an ocean of winks, she put it out of her mind. Which is why it was even more of a surprise to find herself on a date with 'Beardy Will' just a few days later.

In his profile, Will suggested he liked to 'wine and dine'. Claire was impressed when they'd arrived at a beautiful restaurant on the outskirts of town. It was rustic yet stylish; all wrought iron and wood, with a huge open fireplace and cosy beams on the ceiling. Claire had never been anywhere like it before. It was exciting, and she began to enjoy herself.

They ordered their meal. The waiter retrieved their menus and left them to it.

'You look beautiful tonight, by the way.' Will smiled at Claire across the table. The flickering candlelight made his face look mysterious but alluring.

'Oh, thank you.' Claire smoothed the front of her dress. She'd picked her emerald green velvet number, and it seemed to be doing the trick.

'The colour, it really suits you,' he continued, taking a sip of his wine. 'Green was always Emily's favourite colour.'

'Oh,' said Claire, unsure how to respond. She started to feel a little warm. 'It's mine, too.'

'Mmm,' Will nodded in appreciation, 'you wear it well.' Claire blushes deepened.

They chatted easily about the weather and current affairs, and Claire felt completely at ease. Will talked about creativity and his love of free spirits. Claire tentatively mentioned her knitting, and Will seemed so genuinely interested, it made Claire blush all over again.

By the time their food arrived, Claire was lost under Will's spell. He was charming and gentlemanly; he knew exactly what to say and when to say it. Claire could feel herself swooning. 'This is perfect,' Claire murmured.

'The perfect place for a perfect girl.'

The meal was delicious. Will's taste in restaurants was another plus. Claire didn't set down her cutlery until every last mouthful had gone. Seeing her empty plate, Will smiled. 'I do love a girl who appreciates fine cuisine.'

She dabbed at the corners of her mouth with her napkin. 'Well, I do try.' They both laughed.

'It's good. Makes a nice change. Emily just ordered salads all the time.'

'Do you have a sister?' asked Claire.

'No.' Will shook his head.

Emily. Claire turned the name over in her mind. She was sure he'd said it before, but the evening was going so well... 'Never mind,' she muttered, nodding as he offered her more wine.

'So, come on,' Claire was eager to fill the silence that had now fallen between them, 'why did a guy like you reply to a girl like me?' She wasn't about to reveal the real truth behind her 'wink', but considering how well the date was going, she was curious why Will was still on the market - and more so, what made Claire the fish he'd picked from the ocean.

'Why not? From your profile I could see you were pretty, fun, and genuine. You don't know how hard it is to find a genuine girl these days.'

She smiled. 'You've truly flattered me tonight.'

'Don't mention it. I take pride in my eye for beauty. It's part of my job.'

Suddenly Claire felt ashamed. She'd sat with this man for well over an hour and hadn't even asked such a basic question. 'Oh, my life, how rude of me! Will, what do you do for a living?'

He laughed. 'Don't worry about it. I'm a wedding photographer. Emily always said it was everyone else's love stories that killed my own. But I don't think so. In life, there are givers and takers. I like to think of myself as a giver. What about you?'

'Sorry?' Claire stopped swooning when she heard the name again. 'Who's Emily?'

'Huh?'

'Emily. The lady you keep mentioning. Who is she?'

Will looked baffled. 'I don't remember mentioning an Emily.'

She frowned. 'You did. Just now, about the love stories, and before with the salads.'

'Well, it's a bit of a coincidence...' He drew a long breath, 'but my ex was called Emily. I don't see what she has to do with our evening.' He reached for his glass and took a large gulp of wine, just as the waiter returned to the table. 'Ah, now then.' He looked relieved. 'Pudding?'

At the end of the evening, Will walked Claire to her front door. Conversation had dried up in the taxi; the driver even turned up his radio to diffuse the awkwardness. All Claire wanted was to get indoors and crawl into bed.

If this guy is so hung up on his ex, why is he dating? I doubt he's short of offers, but if he can't get her off his mind, what's he waiting for? He should follow his heart.

Pondering the thought, she didn't notice Will's lips edging towards her. She snapped back to reality when their noses touched.

'Oh,' Claire gasped. She couldn't do it. Kissing a man who'd spent the night talking about his ex, and who she knew she'd never see again, just seemed wrong. She flinched, and a few strands of her hair snagged in Will's beard. Claire flapped, trying to tug her hair free, whilst Will tried to hold onto her upper arms before she pulled them both over. When they finally detangled, they stared at each other, neither entirely sure what had happened.

'Well... I've had a lovely evening.' His words sounded forced.

'Um...' Claire couldn't believe he was still trying.

'Thank you…erm…' She could see the panic in Will's eyes. 'Sorry, I've never been very good with names.'

She was astounded. Just when she'd thought the situation couldn't get any worse. 'Claire,' she snapped. 'My name is Claire.'

'Well, goodnight, Claire.' Will gave a small bow - obviously not knowing how else to depart after such a shambles - before briskly turning on his heel.

*

The next morning, Claire had an epiphany. If she'd wanted a boyfriend that badly she would have seen past Dan's poor date choice, Ben's table manners and Will's ex. The problem wasn't the lack of a boyfriend. She wasn't missing snuggles on the sofa, or fancy date nights. She missed the person she used to be.

The Claire that had been with Muscles at least had purpose, a secure job, a long-term relationship, and a hobby. She'd been complete. Ever since the split, nothing had been the same for Claire; her emotions, her focus, her knitting… they'd all gone to pot.

Her feelings for Muscles had never been that strong. She had no excuse not to move onwards and upwards.

Claire knew where to start. As much as she tried to ignore it, the root of more than one problem lay in a bag in the corner of her bedroom, gathering dust.

Since she'd taken Lissy to the Stitch and Bitch session, when she'd unsuccessfully tried to woo Adrian, she'd not been back. That was three weeks ago.

She'd been busy with her failed dates, yes, but if she was honest, the main reason was because it was easier to avoid Adrian than continue their friendship.

But it was time Claire faced her demons – all of them. Tomorrow was Tuesday. From now on, that day would be sacred, singled out in Claire's diary (not that this was difficult) for the Stitch and Bitch…

Chapter Eleven

"Friends are the stepping stones to happiness"

As she got dressed the following morning, Claire booted up her laptop. *If I'm being serious about this 'independent woman' thing, that dating profile has to go.*

The page loaded and Claire's cursor found itself at the search bar; her fingers couldn't resist. She typed a username, and was shocked to discover that OddBall101 was nowhere to be found.

Claire changed tack and searched for anyone called Adrian in the surrounding area. She found bald Adrians, blonde Adrians, old Adrians and teenage Adrians, but no wool-shop-owning, crazy-scarf-wearing, gangly Adrians. Claire pushed the laptop away and huffed in defeat.

Adrian doesn't need a dating profile, because obviously, he's no longer single. She let the thought dwell for a second whilst glaring angrily at her laptop, but shook it away and breathed deeply. Today wasn't about Adrian. Not wanting to waste a moment more, Claire clicked the relevant buttons and terminated her FishTank account.

During the last few weeks Claire hadn't seen Adrian. Neither had she heard from him. The best way to describe their communication was like a flurry of snow: initially, it had been thick and fast; now spring was around the corner, it was as if it had never happened at all. Claire felt gloomy at the thought. It was time to let it go. And to make herself, and more so, her knitting, number one priority.

Just before 2pm that day Claire loitered round the corner from Oddballs. With her mind empty of uncomfortable thoughts concerning Adrian's love life, she felt guilty for abandoning the Bitches.

And now she expected them to take her back into their group without a murmur. They'd been nothing but kind to her in the short time she'd known them.

She mithered outside, not entirely sure what she should do. She was committed to tackling her woolly demons, but she couldn't be sure these ladies would be overly willing to help her.

She edged around the corner and peered through the shop window, hoping there'd be a sign that would help her decide what to do next. She saw Adrian busy with a customer, so she pressed her face to the glass to see through to the back of the shop.

As her eyes focused she could hardly believe what she saw. Sat at the large table was Lissy. The fashionista, who'd 'never touched a pair of knitting needles in her life before'. The session was yet to start, but Lissy already had needles in her hand and was knitting, fluently.

Doreen's needles were also furiously clicking away, though neither knitter glanced at their work. At one point, Doreen must have said something funny, because Lissy threw her head back with laughter - even then, she didn't lose a stitch. Claire's worries instantly evaporated and she strode through the door.

Knitting had always been Claire's 'thing', and there was no stronger motivation to conquer her yarn-based problems than seeing her friend excelling at *her* hobby. *If Lissy can do this, so can I!*

Claire's fears proved unfounded. As she marched towards the large table she was met by a plethora of beaming smiles and wide grins.

'Claire!'

'Oh, Claire, how lovely to see you.'

'I'm so glad you're back!'

'Hello, my dear! Take a seat.'

Claire looked at Rene's spindly hand tapping the seat beside her and she instantly relaxed. She took the seat gratefully, and pulled her knitting enthusiastically out of her bag. She was happy to be back but knew she owed them some sort of explanation. She cleared her throat. 'Hi, everyone, sorry I haven't shown my face in a while. You see…'

'It's okay, the ladies know. I filled them in while you were, er, absent,' Lissy interrupted.

'What?' Claire was confused.

'They're all for it,' Lissy whispered. Then louder, 'We're all on board, aren't we, ladies?'

'Oh, yes!' Beryl waved her phone around, beaming. 'We've been exchanging textual messages all about it.'

Claire's eyebrows knitted together. *Why on earth would these ladies be happy that she abandoned them to go on some silly dates? And why would they text each other about it?* It didn't make sense.

Lissy put her knitting down and pointed towards Adrian whilst he saw to his customer. She drew a heart in the air then gave Claire a thumbs up. A chorus of girly giggles erupted from the Bitches. Claire cringed, finally getting the hint.

'Oh.' Before she had time to say anything, she saw Adrian had wrapped up his sale and was coming over.

'Claire!' he said, with what seemed like genuine surprise. He grinned at her. 'How was your holiday?'

She just stared at him. *Holiday? What holiday?* She couldn't call her string of failed dates a vacation.

Baffled, she paused, then she caught sight of Lissy making circular movements with her hands over Adrian's shoulder. 'Roll with it!' Lissy mouthed. The rest of the women joined in with the impromptu game of charades. Lissy outstretched her arms at her sides, which Claire presumed was the sign for a plane. Doreen wobbled around on her chair, her arms flailing; she was either miming being fanned in a sunny climate, or she was seriously unwell.

Claire turned her attention back to Adrian. 'It was wonderful, thank you. Very warm.' She assumed there would be somewhere in the world that boasted tropical weather in February, but nothing jumped in her mind. 'You know how it is - always good to get a change of scenery,' she rambled.

'Where did you go?' he asked innocently. *Damn!* She racked and racked her brains for a plausible response. Fortunately, the reruns of Family Fortunes she often put on for background noise, whilst trying to get to grips with her knitting, came into fruition - saving her bacon.

'Phuket!' she shrieked, with terrible pronunciation, and as if she was claiming 'house' at bingo.

'I'm sorry?' said Adrian.

'Phuket!' she said again, not quite as shrill. Everyone went quiet. 'Thailand,' she added. 'I went to Thailand.'

'I see.' Adrian didn't look convinced. 'You haven't caught the sun much.'

She saw Gladys touch her knitting then flinch, withdrawing from it sharply. Gladys then pretended to blow on her finger.

'Oh, I, er, try to keep out of the sun. And I wear a high factor sunscreen. I burn terribly.' Claire combed her fingers through her curls. 'Red-head problems.' Gladys gave Claire a thumbs-up behind Adrian's back before picking up her needles again. Claire smiled. She was doing quite well.

'Well, that's a shame. I hope it didn't ruin your holiday too much.'

'Oh no. It was the perfect getaway.' There was an awkward silence. Adrian looked at Claire, and Claire's gaze flitted between him and the ladies around the table.

'Right, well, I'll leave you ladies to carry on then.' Adrian headed to the counter and busied himself.

Claire flaked out in her chair. 'Geez, ladies, a little more warning next time.'

'We didn't get chance!' said Gladys. 'He was too quick. We planned to warn you, but he just pounced. I think he missed you.'

'You did great,' Beryl reassured her.

'You should take up acting, dear!' said Rene. 'Phuket!' she chuckled, which set everyone else off, even Claire.

The session settled down. Needles began clicking away in

a rhythmic staccato. Everybody's needles but Claire's, that is - she spent the first hour trying to untangle her ball of stubborn red wool. She eventually dumped it on the table.

'What's wrong, dear?' said Rene.

Claire sighed. 'To be completely honest, I don't know. Every time I've picked up my knitting lately, I just can't get it right. It doesn't matter what technique I use, what size needles I have, or what pattern I try. It just doesn't work out.'

'Maybe it's the wool, then.' Rene said, nodding towards the bright red mass sprawled across the table. 'Red is a very angry colour.' She rummaged around in her trolley for a moment. 'Here, try this.' She presented Claire with a brand-new ball of mint green wool. 'A fresh start.'

Gratefully, Claire took the plump ball and squeezed it in her hands. It felt heavenly. The mint colour was bright and welcoming, the wool itself was smooth, soft and inviting. Claire didn't want to put it down. This had to be one of the nicest things anyone had ever given her.

The red wool still taunted her on the table. 'What will I do with this now? Trade?' Claire offered it to Rene. 'Though I'm not sure if red is a good colour for a baby.'

'Maybe not right now, but it would come in lovely for a little Christmas number.' Rene happily scooped up the wayward wool and plopped it in her trolley. Claire set about finding the centre of her shiny new ball of wool.

The next half-hour flew by. Claire hadn't realised she'd zoned out of the group conversation until she felt Rene nudging her leg. 'Huh?' She looked up, a little dazed.

'I was just saying that your wool is a beautiful colour,' cooed Doreen. 'What are you making?'

Claire looked down, and was surprised to see a neat strip of knitting on her knee. 'I'm not really sure. I just cast on without thinking, and, well…' She held up her work and admired it silently. 'A scarf, perhaps?'

'Maybe,' Doreen nodded. 'But you've used stocking

stitch – won't that curl without a border? You need something with a bit more texture. What about cable?'

Claire's eye widened. 'Let's not get too carried away! I'm quite happy to have done this.' She knew Doreen meant well, but inside, she was so proud of her achievement, she didn't want to change a thing. The fear of ruining it was too great.

'How about a moss stitch then?' said Adrian, who'd reappeared. He also looked at Claire's knitting with a smile.

She began to feel flustered. The last thing she wanted to do was complicate things again. 'I think it's best I stick to the basics right now. Maybe I'll just fashion this into something else after cast off.' She dropped her head and returned her attention to her knitting, hoping that would end the conversation.

'I could give you a mini masterclass, if you like,' Adrian offered, not taking the hint. 'You've got nothing to be scared of. It looks perfect.' Agreement came from the rest of group and Claire blushed.

'Thank you,' she said quietly.

At 4:15pm Claire saw an opportunity. The Bitches had all got off on time, and Lissy was idly leafing through some knitting patterns at the back of the shop. No one was paying her the least bit of attention, so Claire made her way over to Adrian. *Here goes nothing.*

'Hey.'

'Hey.'

The pair looked at each other for a moment; Claire hadn't actually planned what she should say. As she gazed into Adrian's eyes, she was reminded of how intensely blue they were - like two topazes dazzling in the sunlight. *Say something, idiot!*

'So, erm…about that masterclass?'

Adrian smiled. 'No problem. I can teach you anything you want to know.'

'Oh yes, please. 'I'd really appreciate that,' she said.

'How does tonight sound? I could pick you up around eight?'

'That would be perfect.'

'Brilliant. I'll see you then.' Adrian's smile stretched from ear to ear.

When she relayed the conversation to Lissy during the drive home, she watched her friend dissolve into giggles. 'You go, girl!'

'What are you laughing at?' Claire began to laugh, too.

'That's more like my Claire-bear!' said Lissy.

'It's only a knitting class.'

'Yeah, right,' Lissy playfully pushed Claire's arm.

'He's got a girlfriend.'

Lissy looked offended. 'Adrian? A girlfriend?'

'Yes! Abi.'

'What? The girl from the Trout?' Lissy laughed again. 'During the last three Stitch and Bitch sessions, he never mentioned her once, despite the ladies grilling him for gossip. Seriously, there's no girlfriend. Go! Have fun!'

Claire wasn't totally convinced. But then Adrian had initiated their 'masterclass' that night. *Would he do that if he had a girlfriend who may disapprove of such an invitation?* She had no idea what Adrian thought. At the end of the day, all she expected to do was improve her knitting skills. And to clarify a thing or two. Maybe.

Chapter Twelve

"Mood swings can be positive and negative. Ride the highs"

'I didn't go to Thailand,' Claire blurted, as Adrian unlocked his front door.

'I guessed as much.' Adrian smiled. In fact, he'd not stopped smiling since he'd opened the passenger door for her, outside her parents' house.

During the car ride, it was as if the last few weeks had never happened. The pair had chatted effortlessly, like old friends. Claire was so relaxed, she felt she had to confess. 'How? I thought I had you fooled.'

'I don't miss anything within those four walls, Claire. I think you and the ladies deserve an Oscar, though.'

They stepped inside the house. Claire, engaged in their conversation, didn't look where she was going; she bumped into an enormous bouquet of fresh, white lilies that were perched on one of the bookcases nearest the door.

She watched, horrified, as the vase began to wobble. Adrian dived past her to catch them before they crashed to the floor.

'Oh, I'm so sorry.'

'It's o-o-o-' Adrian stammered, before letting out an explosive sneeze. 'Sorry.' He steadied the vase before rushing into the kitchen for a tissue.

Claire took a moment to admire the beautiful lilies she'd nearly sent flying. Their stems were thick and strong, which helped support the cream trumpets. Each petal was long and elegant, curling back at the tip to reveal the bright orange stamens within.

The smell they gave off was quite potent, the kind of fragrance posh department stores bottled.

'Pollen allergy?' She walked into the kitchen and placed a sympathetic hand on Adrian's shoulder. His nose had already started to redden, then he started rubbing his eyes.

She still thought he looked adorable.

'Uh-huh.' Adrian put the tissue to his nose as he sneezed again.

'Oh, bless you. You have got it bad. It's a shame, because they're beautiful lilies. Who are they from?'

'Sorry?'

'The lilies. They're beautiful, but a bit of an odd gift to give a man who suffers from such vicious hayfever!'

'You remember Abi,' Adrian coughed. 'She gave them to me yesterday.'

'Oh.'

'She meant well,' he said. 'I told her about my mum, and I think it must have touched her, because the next thing I know she turns up with those.' He gestured towards the hallway. 'She said no other man would understand why she'd bought flowers, but I would, because I'm sensitive.' He gazed at the floor. 'She's sweet.'

'Hmm,' Claire wasn't so sure. 'Why keep them in the house if they make you ill?'

'I can always take medication. They're too nice to throw away.'

She had to bite her tongue. There was so much more she wanted to say, but instead, she changed the subject. 'I suppose. Anyway…let's get you away from them and get down to business.'

Adrian led Claire into the living room and she settled herself on the sofa. He rummaged around in various baskets that were dotted around the room; she hadn't noticed them last time. The large, round wicker baskets, which sported chunky handles on either side, were lined with vibrant material, in lime green, bright orange or fluorescent pink colours. They each contained a wealth of wool, in many different textures, sizes and shades.

He sat next to her, holding two pairs of knitting needles and a comically large ball of fluffy, burgundy wool. He handed her a set of needles and expertly delved into the centre of the ball, searching for the end of the yarn. 'You know, if you can do stocking stitch, moss stitch is a doddle.'

Claire nodded. She watched as Adrian found the end and began to pull a small amount of the wool through. 'It should offer just enough texture to give that scarf of yours some life. Shall we give it go?'

She nodded again and took the end from him. 'Once upon a time, I could moss stitch.'

'By the end of tonight you'll be a pro,' he assured her.

However much Claire wanted to concentrate on Adrian's tuition, her mind was distracted by Abi's grand gesture. *What do I do now?* She wanted to ask Adrian about Abi, if he liked her…she wanted to know everything. It took a huge amount of self-restraint to keep quiet, and to remain calm and collected, as Adrian asked her to cast on thirty-five stitches. He did the same, after finding the other end of the wool.

'Right…' Adrian cleared his throat. 'Take the needle in your right hand, and put it through the front of the first stitch on your left needle.'

Claire jabbed her needle at the stitch. She prodded and probed relentlessly, and became frustrated that she couldn't complete the task in hand.

'Um, are you alright with that?' asked Adrian. 'Do you need a hand?'

She knew it wasn't just her co-ordination that had gone off course. She couldn't concentrate on her knitting when Adrian was beside her.

Oh, that's it, I can't take it any longer! She had to know. She couldn't carry on with their evening if it was going to be futile. 'Have you seen Abi a lot since your first date then?'

Adrian paused, seemingly shocked by her question when they were trying to master the finer points of knitting. Claire hurriedly poked her needle through her stitch whilst he found his voice.

But he didn't mention Abi; he didn't even divert from his

tutorial. 'Now, take the wool in your right hand…'

'Because I haven't heard you talk about her since then,' Claire prompted.

'…and pass it over the top of your right needle.'

'And you were so excited before you went,' said Claire.

'Then pull your needle back through, that's it.'

'She's pretty, don't you think?'

'Then take the wool from the back of the work to the front.'

'And I know you've deleted your FishTank profile.'

'And get ready to do a purl stitch.'

'And I think you're just ignoring me…'

'Claire!' Adrian looked drained, as if teaching her a simple stitch had taken everything he had. He shook his head in disbelief. 'I thought you came here for a knitting class. Not to interrogate me.'

'Sorry,' She realised she was being terribly ungrateful. He was trying to help her, after all. 'I just thought…' she trailed off.

'Can we *do* now and *think* later?' Adrian said quietly. His eyes pleaded with her.

She nodded and swallowed the lump forming in her throat. 'Yes. Of course. Let's go again.'

After Adrian showed Claire the intricacies of the moss stitch, the pair 'click-clicked' away with their needles for a little while. Claire kicked herself for pushing Adrian to talk about Abi. She realised how childish she'd sounded, but she hadn't been able to stop herself. She didn't want to sound like she was obsessed, but the question of whether Adrian and Abi were an item was burning her up inside. Although keeping her mouth shut was painful, it was what she needed to do.

They completed a few more rows in silence, then Adrian said, 'Is everything okay between us?'

Claire didn't answer. *Isn't that something your partner would ask, if you were in a relationship?* Confused, she decided it would be best if she didn't reply, and instead, appear to be completely engrossed in her knitting.

'I'm sorry if snapped at you,' he added, not fooled by Claire's indifference. 'But you had so many questions, all at once.'

She still didn't know what to say.

'We don't seem to have been the same since my date,' he continued. 'And, tonight, you seem a little preoccupied with Abi. You know, if something's wrong, I'd love to put it right between us.' He paused, then added, 'Because I've, um, missed you, you know.'

Claire heart melted. It had obviously taken a lot of courage to say that. It showed in the way he'd paused mid-sentence, and because he'd needed to take a deep breath before he spoke - and in the way his knitting had picked up pace, because his hands had run away with him. He'd put himself out there, on a metaphorical ledge. Much to Claire's annoyance, in that moment, she had to agree with Abi; Adrian was, indeed, a sensitive soul. His heart was on his sleeve, and she knew he was waiting for her to reply.

'Well, I imagine things are going well between you and Abi. Who am I to intrude?' she mumbled. *That's me in the 'friend zone' forever. Nice one, Claire.*

'Wait, what?' Adrian frowned. 'Me and Abi?' The penny took some time to drop, but eventually he shook his head, the grin back on his face. 'Oh, Claire. Me and Abi…we're just good friends.'

Her face must have looked an utter picture, due to the utter confusion she felt. 'But your date…' She had to stop herself before she blew her cover. How could she admit to stalking the pair of them that night? She couldn't say that she'd actually seen them leave while the night was still young.

'We ended it early, Claire. We got along just fine, but we both agreed there wasn't a spark between us.' Adrian dropped his gaze to his lap.

Claire's stomach felt hollow. Why had it not occurred to her that their date could have been a flop just as much as it could have been a success? *Poor Adrian!* She'd spent the last few weeks distancing herself from him when he probably needed a friend more than anything. She tried to ignore the realisation that she'd been a terrible friend by changing tack. 'So, why delete your FishTank profile if you're still looking?'

He shrugged. 'I didn't see the point, if I'm honest. I only set it up in the first place because you were so keen on the idea. I didn't want to let you down. When we didn't seem to be talking, in conjunction with the fact I wasn't getting any messages from anyone on there, there seemed little point carrying on with it. So, I took my profile down. It was a bit humiliating, to be honest. I'm not a great fan of talking to people over the internet. Too many dangers.'

Just like that, all the questions Claire had agonised over, all the mysteries she'd turned over and over in her mind, they were all solved. Adrian wasn't dating Abi. Adrian was single - and had been all this time. So Adrian had acquired another female in his life, one who was petite, blonde and pretty...that's all they were: friends.

Claire was overjoyed. Even Adrian perked up a bit, like a huge weight had lifted from his shoulders. Neither of them said any more on the subject of relationships; instead, the pair talked non-stop about every other subject under the sun whilst feverishly knitting away.

Neither noticed how quickly the ball of wool had diminished until it was gone. Claire's pace had improved dramatically; with all the excitement, her needles had clicked much faster, to the point where Claire believed smoke might rise from their tips. It was almost as if she was channelling her joy and positive energy into her hands and her needles.

As Claire tried to bring more yarn across her needle she felt tension. She looked across at the wool and saw it had gone, and that the tips of Adrian's needles were almost touching hers. And that the pair of them were now much closer than they were. All that lay between them were the ends of two individual moss stitch scarves. Claire giggled sheepishly.

'Whoops,' Adrian murmured. The room suddenly felt warm. Claire blinked up at him, suddenly lost for words. She could smell Adrian's aftershave and the sweetness of the lilies in the atmosphere. She was giddy; she felt closer to Adrian, after everything they'd shared during the last few hours.

She sensed him leaning in. *He's going to kiss me!*

His slender frame turned towards her, and his neck, bearing one-day-old stubble, extended slightly. The pair were so close that she could feel his warm breath on her lips. She revelled in the feeling, hoping she wouldn't faint from all the excitement. *Surely not. I can't miss this!*

She knew that, if she leaned in a little more, she'd close the gap between them entirely. Her stomach did a summersault, like when she'd been at school discos playing kiss-chase and the cutest boy in school had her cornered. She closed her eyes and moistened her lips in anticipation. *This is it!* She was glad they were sitting down; had they been stood up, her legs would have turned to jelly.

I wonder what kind of kisser he'll be? A sweet pecker? A juicy snogger? A tongue-tangoer?

Without warning, at the moment of impact, Adrian drew in a sharp breath before turning his head and letting out an epic sneeze.

'AATCHOOOOO!'

Claire's eyes flew open. She just caught a glimpse of Adrian scurrying off in the direction of the kitchen. A few seconds later, she heard the trumpet solo that was Adrian violently blowing his nose. *Mood, killed.*

When he returned, he found Claire casting off her stitches with the remainder of the wool. He tentatively sat down next to her and waited until she'd finished. 'Have I ruined this?' he whispered.

'Ruined what?' Claire looked up at Adrian innocently. She saw a pink tinge appear in his cheeks. 'Oh, that? Don't worry about it.' She began gathering her things. 'This masterclass has been amazing. I've learnt a lot.' She got up to retrieve her coat.

Claire wasn't lying. She'd learnt a lot that evening. As she headed for the door, she promised Adrian she'd text him. She politely declined his offer of a lift home and made her way to the bus stop. The moment she boarded, she felt her mobile phone vibrate in her bag.

It was a message from Adrian. *You're right, I should get rid of the lilies. Sorry if I ruined everything. Hope there will be a second chance Xx*

Smiling, Claire did not hesitate to reply. *All good things come to those who wait xx*

Chapter Thirteen

"Creatures of habit never see the universe, only the black holes"

A few weeks later, relations between Adrian and Claire were still going well. Their friendship continued effortlessly; the almost-kiss didn't change a thing. Claire decided not to overthink the near-miss at all. She vowed to simply enjoy life, and not to try and force things. *Whatever will be, will be.* Having Adrian back in her life was more than enough. For now, anyway.

As for her knitting, everything began falling into place. The Bitches had become surrogate grandmas to Claire; she didn't know what she'd do without their crazy banter and cackling choruses. Beryl, Doreen, Rene and Gladys could do nothing but sing her and Lissy's praises, given how far they'd both come in a matter of weeks.

Finally, Claire's tension was perfectly even again, her moss stitch scarf was complete, and she was currently working on a pair of matching gloves. The only holes in sight were those that would eventually accommodate a button. Everything felt like it was on the up, and Claire was loving it. After the difficult few months she'd endured, she thought it was about time she felt joy again.

So, it was a shock when, during a quiet afternoon at the surgery, Doctor Leach perched on the edge of her desk. Claire had sneakily been trying to complete some on-the-job knitting; now her concentration was broken.

Doctor Leach was a gentle giant of a man. He was tall and sturdy with broad shoulders. He had a good physique, for his age, the result of a good diet and lifestyle, just as you'd expect from someone who worked in the health industry. Though not as fit as he once was, time had still been kind.

At sixty-five, wrinkles had begun to take root and the crow's feet at the corners of his eyes were deep, but etched with kindness. Claire thought Doctor Leach was what Santa would look like in the flesh, if he hadn't eaten all the mince pies.

He perched so awkwardly on her desk that she considered offering him a cushion. Whatever his reason for being there, it was doing nothing for his back, and he looked incredibly uncomfortable.

The doctor's eyes seemed greener than usual. He gave Claire his most sympathetic look, the one he usually reserved for the surgery's frequent hypochondriacs.

Though his mouth was relaxed, his laughter lines had an unfamiliar downward angle. Whatever Doctor Leach was about to say, it was serious.

Claire rested her knitting in her lap.

'There's something I need to tell you, Claire,' Doctor Leach began. 'I know it may come as a bit of shock, but once you think about it, you'll realise that it's not much of a shock at all.'

With no hint of what he what he was referring to, Claire suddenly felt uneasy. 'Go on,' she said. Her mouth felt as dry as a desert.

'As a fresh-faced nipper leaving medical school, I never once believed I'd run my own practice,' he said, smiling whimsically. 'It's been absolutely marvellous. But, like all good things, it must come to end.' He choked a little on those last few words. 'The recent decision by the government, regarding NHS funding, has deemed Dovedon Surgery no longer necessary. I wanted you to be one of the first to know.'

'No longer necessary? You mean…'

'They're closing the surgery. We have six months to transfer our patients and tie up any loose ends.' Claire felt like she'd been stabbed through the heart. 'They're making the official announcement at the end of the week,' Doctor Leach added. 'I only had it confirmed this morning.'

She had never hugged Doctor Leach before. Being the

practice owner, and, therefore, her boss all these years, she'd always seen him as a friendly headmaster. He was approachable and smiley, and always there when you needed him, but he carried an air of authority you couldn't ignore. Hugging a man like that never seemed appropriate – until now.

She stood up and flung both arms around him. As she did so, her knitting sprung into the air between them. Some of the yarn became hooked on Doctor Leach's suit buttons, whilst one of the needles punctured the side of her woollen cardigan, hanging loosely between a stitch. When Claire let the doctor go, she was horrified to find they were entangled together. Claire felt tears prick the corners of her eyes, her embarrassment doing nothing to stave them off; she knew she wouldn't be able to keep them back for long.

'I thought I'd let you know now, before the big announcement and all. You've always been a gem, Claire.' Doctor Leach squeezed the top of her arm reassuringly before unhooking himself from his woolly leash.

Doctor Leach was an incredible man, she reflected. He had an honest heart and empathy for others - even when delivering such a bombshell, one that affected him more than most, he was worried about Claire.

If she was honest with herself, she'd admit that her reaction to the news was both unprofessional and embarrassing. But, in the moment, she'd felt as if her foundations were crumbling. It wasn't just her job that was under threat, but the very core of who she was, too. She didn't like it one little bit, and so she let the tears fall freely down her cheeks. Had she been sat at her desk, she'd have probably been able to offload unnoticed, but Doctor Leach was still in front of her. 'Oh, no, my dear. Please don't cry. What is there to cry about?' Doctor Leach patted her back comfortingly. 'Look at it as a new beginning. A fresh start. You've been cooped up here, with stuffy old me, for far too long. A pretty, young girl like you deserves to explore the world - and this is your perfect opportunity.'

'What about our jobs? Everyone will be devastated,' she whispered.

'I've been asked to give you all one of these.' Doctor Leach handed her a piece of paper. 'Doctor Samuel's a young doctor. Runs Blossom Hill practice on the outskirts of the city. They're always looking for new blood. From what I believe, a lot of the people there move on to the city hospital, and beyond. Anyway, he's planning to host a welcome party for our staff, in the hope you might join his practice. Why don't you go along? Take a look?'

Claire looked at the invitation in her hand. It was bright pink with large white writing, quite different from the majority of medical paperwork she came across.

> *Doctor Samuel welcomes you to Blossom Hill surgery!*
> *Come and find out what we're all about on April 1st.*
> *You'd be a fool not to!*

At the bottom was a sketchy image of, presumably, Doctor Samuel, in his doctor's coat and stethoscope. He also wore a pair of black sunglasses and was posing behind a couple of DJ decks.

'I'll have a proper look at that later.' Claire folded the invitation neatly and dropped it into her knitting bag, where it would most likely stay. 'What about you?'

'Me?' Doctor Leach smiled. 'I'm going to enjoy holidays in the sun with my wife, and spend time with the grandchildren. I'm going to live life to the full! You don't think sixty-five is too young an age to retire, do you?' he asked playfully. It seemed, for Doctor Leach, the timing was perfect. Claire only wished she felt the same.

As soon as she began her lunch hour, she called Adrian. 'I'll pick you up when you finish,' he said. His voice was full of concern, which Claire found comforting. He was calming and sympathetic, and completely genuine - exactly what Claire needed him to be, and what Muscles would never have been able to offer. Talking to Adrian for just a few minutes made Claire feel calmer, and helped her work out what she needed to do. She even offered Doctor Leach a smile when he passed through the waiting room.

But as soon as she sat down with Adrian on his sofa, Claire let go. Her tears stung as she described how Doctor Leach had broken the news to her. She added extra details, like the way his jacket shoulder had smelt like lavender, and how they'd spent ten minutes disentangling themselves from her knitting. 'It's now a huge knot,' Claire sighed. 'I don't know if I'll ever be able to face untangling it and starting again.'

'I'm sure it's not that bad.' Adrian soothed, but she shook her head.

She dabbed at her eyes with a tissue he'd passed over. 'Dovedon Surgery is all I've ever known. What will I do without it?' She twisted the tissue in her hands. 'It'll be like putting on a sock, when you're missing the right foot to which it belonged. There's no point having a right sock without the right foot!'

'Claire.' Adrian spoke softly, gently placing a hand on her knee. 'I know right now this feels like the end of the world, but even earthquakes can turn out to be tiny ripples.' She met his gaze. She'd never seen eyes like his. They were, at this moment, two serene pools of blue, brimming with empathy. He snaked one of his long arms around her shoulders and pulled her into a sideways hug. 'I'll take a look at the knot ball later, if you want.' A small smile played on his lips.

'You joke now, but you'll understand when you see it.'

'I guarantee I've seen worse. Trust me.' He grimaced comically and Claire couldn't help letting out a small giggle, despite everything. In that moment, she realised that all she'd needed was someone to listen. Not necessarily someone who would understand or offer any advice. Just someone who'd hear her out, give her a cuddle, and tell her that everything was going to be okay. It was all she'd ever needed, but something she'd never had.

On cue, as if he'd read her mind, Adrian pulled Claire in a little bit closer. He leant his head on hers. 'Don't worry, Claire-bear, everything's going to be just fine.'

*

'Now, take the next five stitches, loop them onto your cable needle and pull them to the back.'

Claire's hands trembled. The cable needle in her right hand felt alien and unfamiliar. As she hooked stitches onto it, she'd never felt so unsure about anything in her life. But with Gladys's eyes on her, she really didn't have much choice but to try. With the surgery closure now officially announced, her work life was currently up in the air. Conquering her cabling fears was the least of her worries.

'Right, that's it. Now ignore those stitches for just a minute and purl the next five from your other needle.' The cable needle, and its lonely five stitches, hung precariously as Claire cautiously continued with her row.

'That's it, you're doing great,' Beryl chimed in.
As sweet as the sentiment was, Claire wasn't listening. Her mind had once again reared up with panic over her uncertain future. If she did nothing, she would be jobless in six months. It was a real pressure.

She completed the last of her five purl stitches and set about returning to her cable needle, but her concentration had been broken. As she brought her needle up to make the purl, her hand knocked the cable needle. The stitches lost their grip and the needle clattered onto the table. 'Oh, Claire,' sighed Gladys. 'We almost had it that time.'

'Never mind.' Beryl's hands gripped her needles tightly, perhaps fearing for her own work after watching Claire's disaster. 'Maybe it'll be fifth time lucky.'

Claire sighed too. 'It's not that. My mind's not with it at the — '

'You'll get there,' interrupted Rene.

'I know. I just think it's a bad time because — '

'Practice makes perfect,' added Gladys.

'It does, but what I'm trying to say is-'

'My first cable wasn't perfect,' Beryl chipped in.

'It's not this!' Claire slammed her hands on the table, her needles making a tinny sound on the wooden surface. Everyone stopped their knitting and looked at her.

'Is everything okay, dear?' Rene placed a hand on Claire's shoulder.

'No,' said Claire, taking a deep breath. 'Everything's not okay at all.'

Adrian appeared at her side. Him just being there automatically made Claire relax a little. 'The government have decided to make even more cuts to the NHS,' he told the ladies. 'And as a result, they're closing Dovedon Surgery.' There were shocked expressions all round.

'Oh, dearie,' Rene sighed.

'When did this come about?' asked Doreen.

'What about all your jobs?' said Beryl.

'Surely they can't do that?' Lissy scowled.

'They can't take away Dovedon Surgery! That's absurd,' Gladys huffed, waving her hands in a dismissive manner.

'I know, ladies, I know,' said Claire. They've given us six months before they close the doors for good. It hasn't really sunk in yet. I'm trying to remain positive. There are opportunities to transfer to other surgeries, and at the moment, I have time on my side. I'm sorry if I'm all over the place,' Claire pointed to the heap of knitting in front of her. 'It's just my mind is somewhere else.' The whole table nodded.

'You should take your mind off your work for now. Let go of some of that stress.' Rene wagged a bony finger at Claire playfully.

'Yes, we'll help you find a distraction or two,' said Gladys. 'Isn't that right, Adie?'

'Of course.' Adrian flashed Claire a grin, which made her heart flutter.

After the sessions had finished, Adrian presented Claire

with a parcel wrapped in brown paper. The label attached read 'Open me later'. Claire gave Adrian a questioning look, but all she got in response was a quick wink before he attended to a customer. She looked down at the parcel in her hands and couldn't resist giving it a small squeeze. It was squishy and soft. *Hmm…*

'Ready to rock 'n' roll?' said Lissy.

'Um, sure,' said Claire, hurriedly shoving the parcel into her knitting bag. Whatever it was, she decided, it was a private matter.

During the ride home, she became more curious about the parcel's contents; she couldn't wait to open it. The minute she was home, she raced up to her bedroom. She tore away the paper before she even took off her jacket, finally revealing its contents.

On seeing what was inside, Claire thought she might cry. Inside was a pair of bright pink, chunky knit socks. They looked incredibly cosy, with their thick stitches and plump texture. She lifted them up to her cheek, which is when she noticed the note hiding underneath them.

In Adrian's sloped, handwriting were the words: *This is for your right foot, because you still have one. P.S. I also made you one for your left foot. I couldn't leave you with an odd sock, could I? A x*

Chapter Fourteen

"We all have ghosts from our past. But never be afraid of them – they've helped make you the person you are today"

'Pretty, pretty please…with a ball of wool and a crochet hook on top?' Adrian's eyes were the size of saucers. 'I promise I'll buy you popcorn and sweets. I'll even let you choose where we sit. You can even choose 3D.'

All Claire had heard from Adrian for the last two weeks concerned the release of Fish Out of Water. A 'guaranteed box office smash', the story told of a threat to the human race, due to monsters suddenly appearing from the sea. These terrifying monsters could mimic the appearance of humans, which made killing them quite difficult.

Though she thought the plot was flimsy at best, and the genre of film wasn't usually her cup of tea, a trip to the cinema with Adrian was not something she wanted to pass up. She'd decided days ago that she'd go with him, but his pleading was too cute.

'So when would the showing be again?'

'Tonight at 8.30pm. I'll pick you up. You don't need to worry about a thing. Does this mean you'll go?' Adrian looked like a child in a sweetshop who'd eaten all the blue Smarties. He was practically bouncing on the spot. Claire nodded. 'Brilliant! I'll pick you up, say, quarter to seven?'

'Quarter to seven? Isn't that a bit early, if the showing's at half-eight?"

'Yeah, well, I can't let you watch blood-sucking merpeople on an empty stomach.'

*

The doorbell rang at seven forty-five precisely. Claire opened the door to find that Adrian had slicked his hair to the side for the occasion. He wore a crisp, white shirt, a charcoal tie, which matched his charcoal suit trousers, and a pair of tan leather lace-up shoes. His outfit was topped off with an intricate cable knit jumper, in a lovely maroon shade.

There was a subtle warmth to the air, with spring just around the corner, yet Adrian still sported his trademark scarf – today, snaking around his slender, stubbly, neck, just three times. Whether this was to allow for greater ventilation, Claire wasn't sure, but she knew that Adrian looked good.

Although neither of them had ever mentioned the word date, it felt like one. Adrian had his best knits on, and Claire had spent the evening trying on every outfit she owned. She eventually settled for a floaty cream blouse and black jeans, with understated black heels and a chunky knit to the knee cardigan. Not too flashy, but feminine and flattering, with a hand knit for good measure. Adrian escorted her to his little Micra, and within a few minutes, they'd arrived at the swish Italian restaurant situated next to the cinema, where Adrian had reserved a table for two.

The restaurant was quite swanky inside. There were rows of tables, each with a bright, white tablecloth and silver cutlery, which gleamed in the dazzling light from the spotlights above. The walls were painted in a passionate red, with pictures of iconic Italian dishes in wooden frames. The décor complimented the aroma of mixed herbs and fresh bread travelling across the restaurant. Claire's appetite stirred instantly. She gave Adrian's arm a squeeze in gratitude. 'This place is beautiful.'

He smiled. 'I wasn't lying when I said I wanted to make sure you were well fed and watered before the film. I'll be honest, I love Italian food.'

'Me too! It smells delicious.'

After they were seated and had ordered their food, Claire sat back and watched Adrian for a moment. For a man with limbs so long and gangly he was graceful and controlled. She watched him place his menu down, before he straightened his shirt collar and brushed his fringe aside. She focused on his long, slender fingers, and how nimbly he laid out his cutlery and flattened his napkin. Claire suddenly had an urge to hold them. She shook the thought and looked for a distraction.

'So, who exactly are these merpeople again, and why do they want to kill us all?' Claire knew he'd be pleased that she'd finally taken an interest in the film. He excitedly described the tentacle-clad sea beasts they were about to see, and their plan for world domination.

When the starters arrived, Claire looked at Adrian's plate with food envy. Though tempting, her olives didn't look quite as appetising as his scrumptious bruschetta. Whilst her plate looked to be filled with bloated peas, his bread was topped with plump, rich tomatoes, and it was positively dripping with melted cheese.

He noticed the look of envy on her face. 'Want to try some?' He picked up his knife and fork and cut Claire a particularly mouth-watering morsel. She didn't think twice; she leaned over and took it. He then brought his hand up to her face to catch a piece of stringy cheese that had clung to her chin. He licked the cheese from his finger; they both giggled at the action. *That was just bliss.*

The rest of the meal continued in much the same fashion; the pair becoming cosier and cosier. 'Accidental' touching and brushes of hands were frequent, and Claire swore their knees were not leant against the other's under the table when they'd first sat down. The offering up of their food for the other to try carried on through all three courses, and as they left the restaurant, Adrian offered Claire the crook of his arm. She took it, happily, not just because her heels were making her feet ache, but also because, after the meal they'd shared, it just felt right.

They got to the cinema well before the film was due to start, which meant they had their pick of the seats. Adrian led her to a couple of seats just off the centre.

As they sat down, Claire realised his choice gave them

the best view in the cinema. 'Perfect seats! You're not just a pretty face,' she joked.

'Well, I do try.'

Slowly, the cinema began to fill up. The audience, she noted, was a mixed bag. There were quite a few guys, in various groups - or just two mates looking to catch the film before everyone else saw it; a number of women, in pairs; and plenty of couples. There were also a few families dotted here and there; with regards to one, she noted, the son looked way too young to watch a fifteen-rated film.

As everyone settled in their seats, Claire watched friends laugh and joke together, families and groups share out sweets and drinks, and couples snuggle up close. Just as the lights dimmed, she snuck one last look at Adrian's face before two hours of darkness descended on them. He faced the screen, but she could still see the twinkle in his eyes and his smile stretched from ear to ear.

The beginning of the film, in her opinion, contained lots of talking but not a lot of action - or sea monsters, for that matter. It was just lots of hushed conversations and panoramic shots of the ocean to a soundtrack of loud, tense music. Her eyes began to wander, and she found herself watching Adrian in the light reflected from the screen. He was completely engrossed, his eyes darting from left to right, scanning the ocean shots for any signs of the cannibalistic merpeople.

His hand rested in an awkward position on the chair arm closest to her. It was palm up, and his long, slender fingers were slightly curled, as if beckoning Claire's fingers to join them. She fought the urge to hold his hand and spent the next twenty minutes flicking between his fingers and the screen. She longed for a scary scene, so that she could pass the whole thing off as fear, if she'd read the signs wrong.

She looked up to see a man transform into a frightening-ly-ugly swamp thing; his skin looked like it was bubbling and boiling, and he grew a plethora of tentacles. This was her moment. She reached out and took Adrian's hand, squeezing it tightly as she watched the monster casually bite someone's head off. He glanced at her and noted the shock on her face, before giving her hand a quick squeeze in return - and he kept hold of it when he returned his attention to the film. Claire grinned. The pair remained like that for most of the film, until Adrian began to clench and unclench his hand.

Confused, Claire let go; just a few seconds later, Adrian used the traditional 'yawn and stretch' trick to wrap his arm round her shoulders instead.

At a particularly grizzly scene, where one of the merpeople graphically devoured one of the main characters, Claire turned into Adrian's body and away from the screen. Unfazed, Adrian planted the softest of kisses on her head. 'It's okay, I've got you,' he whispered. She sighed contentedly.

Claire didn't realise the film had finished until the lights came up and the bodies around her rushed for the exit. She'd rested her head on Adrian's shoulder just before the final sequence, and her view had been obstructed by his jawline for the whole thing. But she hadn't cared; she may have missed the blood and guts but, instead, she'd enjoyed Adrian's musky aroma and the sweet scent of his aftershave.

As they headed to the foyer, Adrian reached for Claire's hand. Her breath hitched with happiness. *It's one thing holding my hand in the dark, but in public? That's a different thing altogether!* Completely absorbed with her mental fangirling, she missed her name being called from across the room. She wasn't even aware someone was striding over to them until their path was blocked.

Looking up, Claire saw the obstacle was none other than Muscles. Instantly, like she'd received an electric shock, she dropped Adrian's hand. Her heart, which had been fluttering away from a mix of excitement and contentment, sunk instantly.

'Hey there, baby, long time no speak.'

Claire just scowled at him. 'Shut it, Pete.' *Why here? Why him? Why now?*

Unperturbed by her less-than-warm welcome, Muscles turned his gaze to Adrian. He looked him up and down before smirking. 'Alright, mate?' he grunted.

'Hello,' Adrian responded curtly.

Muscles turned his attention back to Claire. 'Why haven't you called me? I didn't think it would take you this long.' The smug smirk on his face made her want to reach up and slap him, hard, in the hope it would at least dislodge. She wrinkled her nose. He was wearing that horrible white, ribbed vest he loved so much, the one that had his biceps permanently on parade. As she looked more closely, she noted dark circles under his eyes, and stubble gracing his usually clean-shaven baby face.

'I think you know why that's never going to happen,' she shot back. Muscles pretended to sulk, but Claire wasn't in the market for childish gestures any more. 'You're just an ape. A dumb, blabbering ape!'

She pushed past him - which was quite an achievement, considering his stature - and marched out of the cinema. But Muscles being Muscles couldn't leave it like that. 'That's a shame. I'd been looking forward to it,' he called, his voice cracking up with laughter. The goons from his gym, who'd been waiting outside, patted each other on the back as they howled like a pack of hyenas. Claire wanted to yell at them until she turned blue in face, but knew it would only give them more ammunition. She took a deep breath and carried on walking. Adrian lingered for a second, just to shake his head at Muscles and his cronies. Muscles' eyes locked with Adrian's for a moment - electric blues staring down cold browns - before Adrian broke away to catch up with Claire.

Once in Adrian's car, she began to shake. Adrenaline from the confrontation pulsed through her veins. Silently, Adrian unwound his scarf from his neck and handed it to her. She took it, and used it as a comfort blanket rather than putting it on.

She was not about to let Muscles ruin their beautiful evening. As Adrian started up the car, she began to ramble, in an effort to explain. 'That guy used to be my boyfriend. Ugh, he's so full of himself, it's unbelievable! He's not interested in anything if it doesn't involve a gym, or steroids. He's an ape - all power but no brain. In fact, that's an insult to apes...' Claire's voice fizzled out. *Would Adrian wonder why Muscles looked at her with such distaste? Would this put an end to their relationship before it started? Relationship? Where did that come from? Are we in a relationship?* All she and Adrian had done was hold hands.

She decided not to say any more. She plucked up the courage to glance at Adrian, and saw that he was smiling and shaking his head gently. 'You shouldn't let him get to you like that,' he said.

The hairs on Claire's arms started to rise as she felt herself getting angry. Muscles hadn't 'got' to her. She'd have to actually care about what the ape thought to be offended by his brutish, immature jibes. Did Adrian really think she was bothered? 'Get to me like what?' she snapped.

'Like that.' Adrian was still smiling, which began to irritate her. It wasn't funny. 'He was trying to rile you, and you let him.'

'He hasn't riled me!' Claire again snapped at Adrian before crossing her arms.

'Listen to yourself! He's got to you, which is exactly what he wanted.'

She remained silent. She wanted the conversation to end and wondered if Adrian knew he'd hit a nerve.

Finally, they pulled up outside Claire's house.

'If it's really over,' Adrian turned the engine off and looked her in the eye, 'and I *mean* over, you need to stop the name-calling and point-scoring. If you both live locally, you're bound to bump into each other from time to time.

You need to act like grown-ups, or you'll never move on.'
The look he gave her after he'd said this was patronising, in
her eyes.

'Goodnight, Adrian.' Claire got out of the car swiftly,
dumping his scarf on the passenger seat.

'Oh, come on. Don't take it the wrong—' But his plea went
unheard. Claire had already slammed the car door shut.

Chapter Fifteen

"Sometimes, in life, it's as important to listen as it is to talk"

Throughout the following week, Adrian tried to call Claire twelve times. She didn't answer any of them. She responded to a few of his texts, but communication had been curt.

Adrian was right that Muscles had hit a nerve. The ape's assumption that she'd come crawling back - because he couldn't recognise that healthy relationships were built on genuine feelings and mutual respect - grated. As did Adrian's comment that she should act like a grown-up (so, did he think she was immature, then?).

Men. She was fed up with being belittled. She was supposed to be a strong, confident woman.

On cue, Claire's phone rang again. She'd grown so used to ignoring it over the last few days, she didn't bother to glance at the caller ID until it rung off. When she did pick it up, she saw a missed call from Lissy on the display. Before she could call her back, a text arrived.

Hi, Claire, I was just letting you know I'll be picking you up as usual for the Stitch and Bitch today. There's been a change of plan: different venue, different time. I'll come for you in an hour and explain all en route. Ciao. xx

Claire read the text again. *Different venue?* Just because she wasn't on best terms with Adrian, it had no bearing on the Bitches; why would they meet somewhere other than Oddballs? There must be a good reason, she surmised. *Time to get up, then. Get some answers.*

'So you know how the Bitches promised you a distraction from your work worries?' Lissy had a secretive smile on her face.

'Yes…' Claire said hesitantly.

'Well, today's the day. We're going on a field trip!'

'A field trip?' Claire laughed. 'Where?'

'The ladies wouldn't be very happy with me if I gave away the whole surprise.' Lissy winked then pulled into a parking bay. Claire recognised the hustle and bustle of Burlington train station. Lissy looked at her watch. 'Come on, they'll be arriving any minute now.' Claire followed her into the station.

The Bitches were nowhere to be seen on the platform. Lissy kept checking her watch then she'd wander over to squint at the electronic board. Three trains passed. Still no Bitches.

'They should be here by now. I'll try Beryl again. I hope she's remembered her phone.' Lissy turned her back to make the call; at that moment, the troop arrived as a flustered gaggle, their cardigans slipping off their shoulders, and their pop socks rolling down. Even Rene's trademark fuchsia lipstick was a little smeared at the edges.

'Where have you been?' Lissy whirled round. 'I've been worried sick! You told me you'd be able to get here without issue.'

Beryl looked sheepish. 'I forgot my OAP pass.'

'That was just the first hurdle.' Gladys rolled her eyes, patting her hair flat.

'The gap between the platform and the train was rather large. We had to watch where we put our feet.' Doreen shuddered at the memory.

'And the luggage rack would only hold one of our trolleys.' Rene gestured to the congregation of 'happy shoppers' behind them. 'We had to space them out along the train carriages. We nearly missed the stop, trying to herd them all!'

Claire stifled a giggle as she helped the ladies redress themselves. The tone for the day had already been set. 'So, ladies,' she chimed, when everyone had settled down, 'where exactly are we going?'

'Follow me!' Gladys grabbed her trolley and marched off, leaving the rest of the group to follow. Claire scurried after her. Next to the train station was the Burlington exhibition centre; it soon became apparent that Gladys was heading straight for it.

'Ooh, are we going to see a show?' Claire's eyes lit up.

'Sort of.' Rene winked.

In the exhibition centre's foyer, Gladys rummaged in her happy shopper and produced two bright pink lanyards. 'Here you go, you'll be needing this.' Gladys held one out to Claire, who reached for it, her hands trembling slightly with excitement. She read the ticket attached: *The Burlington Wool Craft Show. One Day Ticket.*

'Surprise!' Beryl trilled.

'Thank you,' said Claire, a little overwhelmed. She took in each of the ladies' Cheshire cat grins. Rene waved her arms, ushering her to go inside.

Claire had never been to a trade show. She had longed to visit one, many times, but she'd never got round to making her dream a reality.

She opened the door and her mouth fell open in awe. It reminded her of the first time she'd walked into Oddballs, but on a much grander scale. *The sheer size of it all!* The arena was usually reserved for pop concerts and comedians, but that day it was awash with row upon row of stalls. Everything a wool crafter could need, under one roof.

From hand-spun yarns, to stitch markers made from real crystals, to quirky knitting bags and tiny labels to sew into your handmade garments. There were thousands of patterns and brands of wool; you could even go away with individually-designed, unique needle toppers, or a pair of personalised wool scissors.

'Welcome to paradise,' Doreen whispered. Claire noticed that she wasn't alone in her appreciation, everyone else sported wide eyes and happy smiles. None of them knew where to look first.

The arena was a hive of activity. People were milling round every stall; the noise in the room sounded like a low rumble. Claire felt excitement in the air, and not just within their small group, who were still huddled in the doorway, people pushing past them all the time.

'Right then, Bitches,' Gladys signalled. 'Bags at the ready.' Claire and Lissy watched as the four Bitches lifted the lids of their happy shopper trolleys before grabbing the handles, their knuckles whitening. 'Eyes on the prizes, my loves, eyes on the prizes. Go!' They zoomed off, leaving the two girls stood in their wake.

They managed to catch up with the Bitches as they swarmed around a lady selling handmade buttons of all colours, shapes and sizes. Claire whispered in Rene's good ear, 'Why the empty happy shoppers?'

Rene looked at her a little confused. 'For the freebies, of course.' She glanced at the small lilac shoulder bag tucked under Claire's arm. 'It's a shame you didn't bring anything bigger.' She turned to peer over Doreen's shoulder.

'We'd better look after this lot.' Lissy said with a grin.

The button stall was manned by a cute wisp of a girl, who wore pastel shades head to toe, finished off by a pale pink oversized bow in her long, brown hair. Her makeup was immaculate, but very pink, and her mascara made her eyes look constantly surprised.

'Do you have any sugar skull buttons?' asked Gladys. 'You know, like in the vintage tattoo kind of style?' The girl didn't seem to understand until she saw Gladys's tattooed knuckles. 'Only I'm currently knitting myself a cardigan, and I think they'd make a lovely feature for the collar.'

'No, I'm sorry, I don't,' the girl replied. 'But I do have these cute daisy buttons I made especially for the show.' She picked up a business card, which had a white daisy button attached to one corner. 'Maybe this will do the trick?' She handed the card to an excited Gladys.

'Ooh, lovely,' cooed Gladys. 'I'll take five, please.'

'Five?' The girl had obviously noted that they were a party of six. 'Is that enough to go around?'

Gladys shook her head and patted the girl on the arm. 'No, five each, dear. How am I supposed to make anything with only one button?' Gladys scooped up a pile of the business cards and began dishing them out. The girl winced then sighed. Arguing with the elderly didn't appear to be something she'd prepared for.

Claire ran her fingers over one of the daisy buttons. It was really pretty, with its cute petals. *I'll keep these for something special.* As the ladies left the stall, Claire shot a smile at the young girl. She gave her a strained smile in return, before rearranging her business card display.

The Bitches moved round the stalls in a methodical manner, going up and down each row in turn. After the button incident, Claire expected more shenanigans, but thankfully, they were relatively well-behaved. They looked over what each stall had to offer and chatted to the stallholders about their current projects, and what they'd love to make in the future.

Claire saw so many beautiful items that she found it hard to pick something out. In the end, she treated herself to some beautiful hand-spun alpaca yarn, which she vowed to save for another special project. Rene found a necklace that was also a row counter; she didn't stop talking about it all afternoon.

The second-from-last stall sold patterns for children's toys. Doreen was drawn to it like a magpie and started leafing through the stock. Over Doreen's shoulder, Beryl spotted a pattern for a woolly pirate, complete with a brown, triangular hat and beaded beard.

She grabbed the pattern from the book and showed it to Claire and Lissy. 'Look! You can knit your own Johnny!' she said, excitedly. The woman manning the stall popped up like a meerkat from behind a table, glaring at them. Claire knew that Beryl was a massive Pirates of the Caribbean fan, but it didn't look like explaining this would wash with the woman, who had a face like thunder. Claire quickly took the pattern from Beryl's grasp and put it on the counter. She mouthed an apology and ushered the ladies away from the stall. Beryl sniggered, suddenly realising what she'd said, though Doreen was rather miffed at being moved on. Thankfully, Lissy steered Doreen towards a beautiful lacework book from the final stall and the incident was forgotten.

When they left for tea and cake later that afternoon, Claire felt dazed. She heard Gladys mumbling about the lack of freebies; she bemoaned that they'd only come away with a load of business cards and flyers (she'd obviously forgotten about the daisy buttons). Rene had managed to talk a sweet gentleman into giving her a free pattern for a hat, though they discovered afterwards it could only be completed using the type of yarn he'd sold.

The Bitches may have had their niggles, but Claire had been amazed by it all. She'd seen so many things she'd never even known existed in the world of wool craft. At one point, she'd even petted a live sheep! The only thing missing from the day was Adrian - because, if it involved wool, he'd become her first thought. She checked her phone; her inbox was empty.

When they arrived back at the train station, Gladys was surprised to see her husband waiting for them in the car. 'I can take two more,' he called in a gruff voice.

'Oh,' said Gladys, looking round. 'But that will leave one of you on the train.' The ladies' eyes darted between each other. No one wanted to travel on their own.

'It's okay,' said Lissy, 'there's room in my car. Rene, you live the closest to me, right?' Rene nodded, thankfully. 'Gladys, can you take Beryl and Doreen?' Gladys nodded.

'Come on, it's starting to get cold,' Gladys's husband called from the car. They quickly exchanged hugs and the group divided. Claire helped Rene into the front seat before climbing into the back of Lissy's car.

'I've meaning to ask you, dear,' said Rene, turning slightly in her seat in an attempt to face Claire. 'How are things going between you and Adie?' Her eyes twinkled. Lissy tactfully kept her eyes on the road.

'Oh, erm…' Claire mumbled, fidgeting in her seat, 'they're kind of not going anywhere.'

'But I thought you were courting!' Rene looked affronted.

'We kind of were…I think.' Claire suddenly found her seatbelt fascinating. 'Something came up.'

Rene shook her head. 'Do you still like him?'

Claire paused for a moment. *Do I still like Adrian?* The thought lingered in her mind. Despite her wounded ego, Claire nodded.

'Whatever it is obviously doesn't matter. Life's too short for silliness,' said Rene.

They chatted about wool and patterns until Lissy pulled up outside Rene's bungalow. Rene turned again to Claire. 'Call him,' she urged. She thanked Lissy and got out of the car. They watched her toddle up her garden path.

'She's right, you know,' added Lissy, looking at Claire through the rear-view mirror, before starting up the engine again.

It was quite late by the time Claire got back. After they'd dropped Rene off, she and Lissy went to their local pub for a bite to eat.

She took a shower and got into bed. She found herself staring at her phone, debating whether she should call Adrian. On one hand, it was late, and the last thing she wanted to do was wake him up. On the other hand, she couldn't get Rene's words out of her mind. *Life is too short!*

She let out a sigh and scrolled through her phone for Adrian's number. She pressed 'call' and nervously waited for him to answer. Adrian typically picked up after a couple of rings; just as Claire thought it would switch to voicemail, he answered.

'Hello.' He sounded breathless.

'Hi,' she started, trying her best to sound natural. 'How

are you?'

'I'm good, thanks. You?'

'Great!' She paused. 'You'll never guess where the Bitches took me today.'

'Oh, yeah, the trade show. Was it good?'

'How do you know?'

'Considering how concerned I would have been when no one turned up to the shop this afternoon, I had to know,' Adrian laughed. 'Plus, Beryl can't keep secrets of any size. They've been exchanging 'textual' messages about it for weeks.'

Claire smiled. *Bless Beryl, and her love of 'textual' messaging!* 'So…how was it?'

'It was fantastic!' she gushed. 'I've never seen so many amazing things under one roof. You'd have loved it.'

'Um, go on.' There was a muffled noise on the line. Claire ignored it, and launched into a summary of everything she'd seen and felt. She'd only managed two sentences when she heard another voice on the other end of the line.

'Ade? Ade, can I borrow you a second?' they called. Claire stopped dead. The voice was female.

'Claire? Are you still there?' said Adrian.

She took a moment before she spoke. 'Um, yes…'

The voice came again. 'Ade!'

'Look, can I call you back later?' Adrian's voice was taut.

Claire was about to ask who needed his attention so badly when the voice called more loudly. 'Ade? Come quick! I think I might be burning something…'

'Look, I've got to go. Bye.' Adrian ended the call before Claire could say another word.

For a few moments she sat on her bed, scowling at the phone. She'd only cooled things with Adrian a few days ago, yet he'd already found another girl to take her place. Claire was more than a little disappointed. He didn't seem the type to do that. *Stuff you, Adrian! Stuff you, men. Who needs any of you?*

She laid back, but when she closed her eyes she couldn't stop thoughts of Adrian floating to the surface. He'd seemed sweet and genuine. His smile, his kind words; the way he'd treated her and held her hand; how he looked after her. The way he'd taken her into his world and helped her overcome her fears. These weren't the traits of a player. As the kind of guy who wore his heart on his sleeve, this seemed uncharacteristic.

Claire sat up again and picked up her phone. She wanted answers.

'Claire! I'm so sorry,' Adrian gushed when he picked up the call. 'I was going to ring you back, but thought it was too late.' Claire glanced at the time. It had gone midnight, but she didn't care.

'Who was with you earlier?' she asked. There was a pause. 'Adrian?' she prompted.

'Abi,' he said, resignedly. 'Why do you ask?'

Claire felt a bitter taste in her mouth. 'No reason. Okay, no worries, everything makes complete sense now. Goodnight, Adrian.'

She moved the phone from her ear, ready to hang up, but heard Adrian shout as she did so. 'Claire, wait!' She put the phone back to her ear, despite her better judgement. 'She was only offering me some advice,' he said. Claire tutted to herself. 'I just wanted to ask her something, that's all. She came over as friend. That's it.'

'Adrian, I heard her. You seemed very cosy…you were cooking together or something.'

'Yes, I cooked her dinner. I can't exactly ask her over then let her starve, can I? She was watching the food for me while I answered your call.'

'I'm not stupid, *Ade*.' Claire put an acidic emphasis on the way Abi had said his name.

She must have pushed some buttons because Adrian's response was full of fire. 'I know you're not! But when you're not talking to me, what am I supposed to do? Claire, I'm good, but I'm not a bloody mind reader! I needed some help and I wasn't getting it from you.'

'We've still been texting!' she shot back.

'Hardly.'

'Even so, why turn to her?'

'Because she's a woman. I thought it might have been a 'woman thing'.'

'A woman thing?! Are you serious? Me and Abi are nothing alike!'

'Well, at least we agree on one thing,' he said, flatly.

Claire drew a breath sharply. 'Fine,' she spat. 'I hope you enjoy your life together.'

'Claire! Claire, listen. It's not like that...' But she was no longer listening. She pushed the button and ended the call.

Chapter Sixteen

"First impressions always count"

The next morning, Claire was getting ready for work when a flash of pink crossed her peripheral vision. Focusing on what had caught her eye, she realised it was the leaflet from Blossom Hill Surgery. She plucked it from her corkboard, sighed, then sat at her desk.

The first of April? That must be coming up. Her eyes followed the neat row of crosses that marked days passed on her calendar. They stopped one square from the end of the page. Claire swallowed. Today was the 31st March. The six-month timeframe she'd had to try and combat redundancy was now a five-month timeframe. Her future plans were still as clear as mud.

The trade show had been a welcome distraction, as had been her brief 'thing' with Adrian (*was it even a thing?!*). She'd let time pass her by. The invite she held was an opportunity, one that would have a big effect on her life, yet all she'd been able to think about when she woke was whether Adrian had tried to call her back.

It was time for Claire to embrace the inevitable. She folded the leaflet and dropped it in her handbag. *What have I got to lose?*

*

In the staff-room someone had moved Blossom Hill's flyer to the centre of the noticeboard. Despite the evening being almost upon them, no one looked at it directly. Maybe they thought if they were caught looking, it would be seen as an act of treason.

When Claire went on her lunch break she was relieved to be alone in the kitchen. The solitude didn't last long. One of the drop-in nurses leant over her shoulder and whispered in her ear. 'What are you wearing tomorrow night?'

Claire jumped. 'W-who says I'm going?' she stuttered.

The nurse sighed. 'Because we all are, just no one wants to admit it. It would be daft not to, in my opinion.' She whispered again. 'Everyone's scared because the positions are limited.'

'Limited?' Claire's forehead creased. *I hadn't thought of that.*

'Yeah, you know, just a few jobs; the place is already staffed, remember? There might not be much room at the inn, if you catch my drift. Everyone's bracing themselves for a dog-eat-dog situation, but I reckon Blossom Hill will thrive with an extra pair of hands or two.' She smiled at Claire. 'I'm sure there'll be room for another receptionist. Hey, did you know Doctor Samuel is one of the youngest GPs in our area?' She winked.

The last thing I need right now is more man drama. Claire mustered a smile, regardless.

'So....' the nurse continued, 'what are you wearing?'

'Oh, I don't know,' mumbled Claire. She hadn't even given it a thought. 'A dress of some kind.'

Hours later, Claire stood in front of her bedroom mirror, fretting. She rummaged through the pile of dresses, blouses and flouncy skirts she'd dumped in front of the mirror, in some vain hope of finding a suitable outfit. One by one she snatched up the garments, held them against her frame for a brief second, then threw them onto the bed with disgust. *Clashing prints are a no-no this season! Would polka dots make the right first impression? Whatever made me buy THAT...such a hideous shade of green. What was I thinking?!* Soon, Claire's bed was no longer visible under the mountain of clothes.

'Aarrggh!' Claire let out an exasperated roar. She had absolutely nothing to wear.

Her phone began to vibrate on the dressing table. She reached over and saw Adrian's name lighting up the display. Without hesitation, she turned it upside down and returned her attention to her wardrobe. The rail was bare. *What to wear...*

She sighed, then her eyes fell on a large bin-bag stashed at the back. Claire felt like she was reaching into Narnia to retrieve it. *What could this be?*

On first sight, it jogged no memories whatsoever. *A bag of unwanted items for charity, perhaps?* Claire untied the knot at the top and let out a gasp. Inside was a mass of tweed knitting, in a rich russet colour. *I remember this!* Claire lifted the garment carefully and revealed the bodice of a jumper dress. Two intricately woven cables graced the front and back, flecks in the tweed adding extra dimensions and beauty to the vines. As she remembered creating the piece, Claire stroked the cables lovingly.

She laid the dress on the mound of clothes and delved back into the bag. In it, she found the two sleeves the dress was missing – although detached, both were finished. There was also a part-used ball of the russet wool and the knitting pattern. Claire scooped up the latter. She was heartened to find she'd left a pencil mark at the end of the sleeve section. Claire skimmed over the rest of the words, her eyes growing wider the more she read. She looked at her watch. She had forty-five minutes until her bus. Forty-five minutes to attach the sleeves, pick up more than a hundred stitches, and knit a ribbed collar. Given the state of her knitting recently, this would be her biggest challenge yet.

Her eyes narrowed. She glanced over at the jumper dress sitting atop the mountain of discarded outfits and fished in the bottom of the bag to see if it held anything else. Her heart skipped a beat as her hands curled around a pair of 6mm needles lurking at the bottom. *Bring it on!*

When Claire entered the function room Blossom Hill had rented for the welcome event, she felt more confident about the whole work 'situation'. So much so, she didn't walk into the room, she strutted. She glanced around the room, and made eye contact with as many people as she could in a few seconds.

Her knitting had turned out beautifully, though picking

up the stitches had been fiddly, and the sewing together had been time-consuming. Teamed with a white shirt, black leggings and black knee-high boots, Claire felt her outfit had the potential to turn heads, and she couldn't wait to show off her creation.

The evening began pleasantly enough. Most of her colleagues from Dovedon Surgery had made the effort to come, and they chatted politely whilst sipping the free wine. Claire took a tour of the room. It had been cleverly decorated, if luring Doctor Leach's staff was the aim; pinned to the walls were various articles and tit-bits about the history of Blossom Hill, as well as its various achievements within the community, and the part the surgery would play in the future of medicine. There was also a number of patients' case studies dotted around – made anonymous, of course – along with gushing praise from Blossom Hill staff members. They spoke in detail about their 'journey', and described how wonderful it was to work there. Claire was disappointed, however, that none of the employees featured were ever tasked with reception.

An hour into the event, and a few people made speeches. Even Doctor Leach took to the stage to say a little about Dovedon Surgery. He thanked his staff for all they'd done. 'I hope all your futures are a great success, and I look forward to reading about each of you in Doctors Weekly. I've only got five years' subscription left, though, so no pressure.' There was a rumble of laughter, and as he stepped down, he received a rapturous applause. The buffet opened then, much to everyone's delight.

Claire joined the queue, and found herself in-between Janet, one of Dovedon's longest-serving nurses, and Daniel, the paediatrician. 'Ooh, Claire. You look lovely,' Janet cooed. 'Where's your dress from?'

'Thank you. I made it myself.' She beamed. Janet and Daniel gave nods of approval.

'It's wonderful. Well done you!' Janet leaned in a little.

'I'm glad you've come. No one was sure if you would. Ever since I heard the surgery was closing, I've been wondering what your plans might be. I mean, as a receptionist, you could go anywhere. Are you planning on sticking with medicine, then?'

Claire had purposely filled her mouth with a mini sausage roll, so that she could get away with just a nod in response.

Once the food had been picked over, champagne was brought round. Claire looked at the flute she'd been handed and lifted it to her nose. She sniffed sharply. *Definitely champagne.*

Janet smiled at the expression on her face. 'I've heard it's this Doctor Samuel. He's doesn't do anything by half, apparently.'

When everyone's bellies were full, and the final flutes of champagne had been handed out, there came a strange crackle. Feedback echoed from the speakers. A booming voice announced, 'Ladies and gentlemen, please give a warm welcome to your favourite doc...Doctor J Samuel!'

An enthusiastic round of applause ensued, though Claire could have sworn the noise emanated from the speakers; the restrained ovation the audience in the room gave wouldn't have exactly broken the sound barrier.

Doctor Samuel appeared on stage. He was quite young - much younger than Claire had expected. He looked fresh from medical school, rather than someone she'd imagined ran their own surgery. His blonde hair was slicked back, and he wore a slim-fitting, pale grey suit. His trousers looked a little short; Claire swore she could see his ankle bones peeking out from the top of his shoes. *No socks?!*

'Hello, everyone, and thank you for coming. I'm so glad you could make it this evening...' Claire wasn't listening; there was something about watching Doctor Samuel's ankle bones dance about the stage she found hypnotising.

Eventually, she tore her eyes from the monstrosity, just in

time to catch the final words of his speech.

'And I can't wait to look after Doctor Leach's "babies". I'm honoured to be following in such a great man's footsteps. I'll try not to drop you on your heads… I joke, I joke!' No one laughed. Claire expected to see tumbleweed blowing across the floor.

Doctor Leach stepped forward to save the moment. 'I propose a toast,' he said. 'To new beginnings!'

'New beginnings,' everyone chorused.

Speeches complete, guests dissolved into factions. Claire joined a small group made up of non-medical staff from both surgeries, as well as a couple of people who worked in the local pharmacy. She was pleased to find that the woman to her left was one of Blossom Hill's current receptionists, a lovely lady named Jill.

Unfortunately, their group was nearest to the stage door. Within minutes, Doctor Samuel was upon them. He squeezed his way into their circle and began telling them his entire life story. 'My mother was confused when I said I wanted to be a doctor. She said I had the looks and charisma of a top model.' He paused for effect. 'But I've always loved helping others…giving a little piece of me to everyone else, so that they can be happy, you know.' He nudged Claire, a wide grin across his face.

She looked up at him. His gaze was hot; she could feel the heat burning into her skull. It felt as if he was trying to scan her mind and figure her out in an instant.

After a few moments, he snapped his eyes away. Interrupting everyone's conversation, he addressed the whole group. 'I just had to get out of my last surgery. The receptionist there adored me, and it didn't go down well with the boss. She was a tad unprofessional…she used to call me 'Doctor Sexual'! When I told her I was leaving to run Blossom Hill she claimed she had heartburn.' He lowered his voice into an exaggerated whisper, 'I think it was code for something else.' More loudly, he added, 'So, I prescribed some indigestion tablets and sent her on her way!' He began to laugh, snorting away to himself. No one joined in. They just watched him, aghast.

'Don't worry, Doctor Samuel, there won't be any heart-break with us. We're not a hotel.' Claire's words came out more venomous than intended, but he didn't seem to notice.

'Oh, heartbreak hotel! Very good, very good!' Claire felt his hand give her bottom a tap. She jumped, not expecting it, then took a step away from him; he was too busy snort-ing to realise. He continued to 'joke' and brag for another twenty minutes, leaning on Jill's shoulder, and accidentally spilling his champagne down the front of her red blouse - numerous times, without apology. Claire eventually man-aged to sneak away when she felt her phone vibrate. She excused herself, claiming it was an important call.

In the hallway, she found a text from Adrian: *Please answer my calls. A x*

She looked at the notifications and saw she'd had twenty missed calls, all from him. She returned her phone to her bag and went back to the gathering.

From the doorway, Claire watched Doctor Samuel make his way to Janet. He put his arm around her shoulders, and started rattling away to her. She looked up at him dreamily. Claire shuddered and turned on her heel. *Maybe Blossom Hill isn't the place for me, after all.*

The streetlamps offered only a dull glow as she stepped into the dark night. Large raindrops fell, which soaked her almost instantly. Keeping her head down, she marched in the direction of the main road, praying that the bus stop wasn't far away.

As she strode through the rain, she was vaguely aware of a car slowing. She raised her head to glare at the driver, expecting to be splashed as it drove through a huge puddle; as she did so, she noticed it was a small, white Micra.

Adrian leant over and wound the window down. 'If the wind changes, you'll stay like that!'

Claire hesitated, then put her head back down and continued to walk.

'Hey!' he shouted. 'Come back.' He nudged the car forward.

'Go home, Adrian,' said Claire. She was tired. The Blossom Hill evening hadn't been the opportunity she'd hoped, and given that she was completely sodden, there was little wonder her voice was curt.

'Don't be silly, you'll get soaked,' he persisted. A particularly large raindrop trickled down her spine, which made her shudder. Adrian pushed the passenger door open; Claire caved and climbed inside.

For a while the pair travelled in silence. 'So…' Adrian said eventually, but Claire interrupted.

'Before you start, I'm only sat here because it's raining.' Adrian glanced at her and a small smile spread across his lips. Claire's usually bouncy hair was flat to her head, and the wool of her jumper dress had started to stretch from the weight of the rainwater it held.

'So… you don't want to talk about the other night, then?' he suggested.

She shook her head. 'No. It's none of my business.'

Adrian paused for second, then said, 'Okay. But I'd rather clear the air.'

She shook her head again. They remained silent.

'So, what's the new doctor like?' he asked after a few minutes.

Claire raised her eyebrows. 'You remembered?'

He laughed. 'Yes, I remembered. It was also how I knew you'd be wandering the streets of Burlington at this hour.'

'He's… okay.' It was clear by the tone of her voice the doctor was anything but okay.

'Ooh, that doesn't sound good.'

'It's fine. Everything's fine.' Claire shrugged it off and the silence returned.

After a good few minutes, Adrian tried again. 'So…'

'I swear to God, Adrian, if you say 'so' one more time…!'

'So...rry.' He grinned.

Claire elbowed him lightly. She couldn't stop a smile creeping onto her own lips.

'You look lovely, by the way,' he added.

She looked at him with scorn. 'Are you taking the piss?'

He shook his head. 'Well, obviously, I'm not referring to "the wet look". But what you're wearing is a stunning piece of work. And you wear it well.' Claire saw his cheeks turn slightly pink.

She looked down at her dress. Despite the fact it had turned into a woolly sponge, there was no mistaking the craftsmanship that had gone into it, nor how stunning a piece it really was. With its intricate cabling, bold colour and unusual design, it was certainly something to admire.

'I remember when you told me you couldn't knit.' His tongue did that thing again, where it just bobbed out between his teeth, playfully.

Claire's smile faltered. 'This is something I made a while ago.'

He shrugged. 'You still made it.'

For the remainder of the journey, they talked about their greatest creations, woolly and otherwise. Claire felt in her element, and described loads of successful projects. She tried hard to remain frosty with Adrian, but she couldn't help thawing.

Adrian told of the world record he and his mother thought they'd broken (for knitting the world's longest scarf, unsurprisingly. They later found out that another knitter had smashed their attempt with a scarf half an inch longer). They arrived at Claire's house. 'Here you are. Home, safe and sound.'

'Thank you.' Claire was genuinely grateful.

'You're welcome.' He paused. 'Before you go, to clarify, are we talking again? Will I see you at the shop tomorrow? Are we…um, friends?'

'Don't push your luck,' was her response, but she smiled. Taking Adrian completely by surprise, she leant over and planted the softest of kisses on his left cheek. As she did so, she breathed in familiar scents of home baking and fresh laundry. Then she detected another scent, a more powerful one. It was rich and sickly, the type that she found hard to rid from her nose, and which made her whole face itch. She tried hard to place it, then realised the floral fragrance clinging to the fibres of Adrian's woollen overcoat smelled a lot like Abi's lilies. She drew back quickly, like she'd been stung.

'Goodnight,' Adrian whispered.

She just about managed to say the same as she got out of the car.

Chapter Seventeen

"Everything has to start somewhere"

When Claire picked up the phone the next day, she knew there was only one reason Lissy was calling.

'So, how did it go?' her friend prompted.

Typical Lissy. Lovely, but impatient. 'Shouldn't you be working?' Claire asked her. It was, after all, 11am on a Friday morning.

'I am,' said Lissy. 'I'm making a very important business call. Because it's very important I know all of my friend's business.'

Claire laughed. 'I can't argue with that.'

'So...spill,' Lissy prompted again. 'Was Doctor Sammie a hottie?'

Claire turned up her nose at the suggestion. 'Oh God, no! Lissy, he's a right knob.' Lissy burst out laughing. 'It's not funny!' Claire protested. 'Last night was awful. He acted like he was a rock star, not a local GP! And he didn't wear any socks!' She could have forgiven that small detail if he'd had jeans on. *But with a suit?!* Claire shuddered at the memory. 'I don't even know why I went.'

She heard a sigh down the phone. 'What man isn't a knob these days?' Lissy observed.

Claire gave it a brief thought. Her mind flitted first to Doctor Samuel, then Muscles, then Adrian. 'You can say that again.'

'You're just looking at this from the wrong angle,' Lissy assured her. 'This is a great opportunity for you. So what if the new doctor is a knob? Within six months you'll be out of there, working somewhere bigger and better. Then the same again six months after that. This is your time to shine, Claire, Blossom Hill is just a pit stop. In the grand scheme of things, what does it matter if he's a prat? He'll not register in your memory when you're the receptionist at Vogue.'

Claire let out a snort. 'I mean it. Don't let this opportunity pass you by because of one guy. This is your chance to get out and see the world. Dovedon's a ghost town, it's time to leave it behind. You need to start looking after number one - and you need to start looking after number one today.'

Claire hesitated before replying to Lissy's speech. Change and moving forward were supposed to be exciting concepts, but if she was honest with herself, she was terrified.

Maybe Lissy was right. Maybe she was looking at it all from the wrong angle. 'I suppose so,' Claire said quietly.

'Yes!' Lissy cheered. 'Go get 'em, girl! Show them who's boss, and start climbing that success ladder. Woohoo!' Claire could just imagine Lissy spinning around in her office chair, punching the air. 'Oh, got to go.' Lissy's voice turned into a whisper. 'Boss on the prowl. But seriously, go for it, you've nothing to lose. I'll catch you later, okay? Ciao!' The line went dead.

For the rest of the morning, Claire thought seriously about her future. The cloud of uncertainty hanging over her wasn't going to clear on its own, or through fate, she concluded. She had to do something about it. She needed to take control, start making decisions. Just bumbling through the day wasn't enough anymore. She had to wake up, grow up, and actually begin to live life like an adult.

These thoughts carried her through the rest of the day, even at tea-time, where she chased the same pea around her plate for ages. As she embarked on the fifth lap, she heard her dad's gruff voice. 'Penny for your thoughts?'

'Is it boy trouble?' her mum suggested.

'Huh?' Claire looked up. 'Oh no, nothing like that. I'm just thinking about my future.'

'You're going to Blossom Hill, aren't you?' said her mum. 'It has ties with the city hospital, you know. Don't worry, you'll be fine.' She waved her hand dismissively, as if the problem was sorted.

'Blossom Hill is the other side of Burlington, though,

Mum. The commute every day will be insane! I need to think about my options.'

She saw her parents exchange a look. Her mother's eyes lit up. 'I knew this day would come!' she sang. 'George, George! Fetch the hamper!'

Claire's dad sloped out of the room. She turned to her mother, confused. 'There comes a time,' her mum began, 'when every woman decides to fly the nest. Whether it's for self-growth, for a career, for a family…for love - it doesn't matter. It's all part of growing up.' Claire's eyes widened. *What the hell is going on?!*

Her mum continued, 'Over the past few years your father and I have been giving this a lot of thought. And we've something for you.' Claire's dad reappeared; he carried what appeared to be a washing-up bowl wrapped in cellophane. He plonked it on her lap.

Claire noticed a thin layer of dust on top of the cellophane and wondered how long they'd been nurturing the gift. 'We want to make sure any transition is as smooth as possible,' her mother reassured her. 'We thought a new home starter kit would come in very useful.' Claire brushed the dust aside and saw that the bowl contained a pair of rubber gloves, a scrubbing brush, a tin opener, and a small plaque that read 'Home Sweet Home'.

'George…' Claire's mum nudged her husband.

'Oh, ahem,' he coughed. 'And we'll pay your first month's rent. So you can settle in without any fuss.' Claire looked up at them, her eyes like saucers.

'Umm…thank you.' She felt overwhelmed. This was not how she expected the conversation to turn out. On reflection, though, perhaps moving closer to Burlington was the perfect solution. And after her parents' enthusiastic speech, she didn't want to tell them they'd got the wrong end of the stick. In fact, the more she looked at the gift-wrapped bowl in her lap, the more she warmed to the idea. 'You seem to have given this a lot of thought,' she said.

'We just want the best for you, dear. The best possible start.' Her mum took hold of her hands and gave them a gentle squeeze. 'You find the flat, house…whatever you fancy. And we'll help with the rest.'

Her mother's face was relaxed, her mouth displaying a warm smile. Her father was smiling too, and nodding at her with eager encouragement. Claire's mind was in overdrive. *Am I ready for this? Is this what I want?* She looked again at her smiling parents and gently squeezed her mother's hands back.

*

A few days later, Claire sat in front of the family's computer in her father's reclaimed study. In the months since Muscles' departure, her father had beavered away to return the room to its former glory. The bookcases had been painted, the leather chairs had come back down from the attic, and a newly-purchased drinks globe took pride of place.

'Here you are, dear. A nice cup of tea.' Her mum whipped out a coaster from nowhere and placed a steaming mug on the desk.

'Thanks,' said Claire, a little distractedly, her eyes still on the screen.

'How's it going?' her mum enquired, settling herself in a chair just behind her.

'I'm just looking at some properties.' Claire concentrated on the screen, though she knew her mum had joined her from the loud slurping noises she made as she drank her tea. As Claire clicked on the images for a certain property she heard a shriek. She nearly hit the ceiling with fright. *What the…?!*

'Oh, not that one, dear!' her mum said with horror, as she peered over her daughter's shoulder. 'The kitchen is way too small!' Claire turned to berate her mother for scaring her half to death. But her mum was on her feet, jabbing a perfectly manicured finger at the screen. 'Just look!'

Claire sighed and returned her attention to the computer

screen. They both tilted their heads to one side for a fresh perspective. 'It *is* a bit small,' Claire conceded.

'It's definitely too small. You can't entertain your new city hospital friends in a poky kitchen like that! No, no, darling.'

Claire clicked onto a different property.

'Open plan!' Her mother's voice raised an octave. 'I couldn't have *my* bedroom in the same room as the kitchen.' Without a word, Claire changed property again.

'Oh, good lord! No off road parking?!'

Claire turned to look at her mother. 'What difference does it make? I don't drive.'

'That's not the point,' her mother said, indignant. 'You still deserve the right.'

Claire rolled her eyes and got up from the seat. 'Thanks for all your help, Mum.' She gently ushered her mother towards the study door. 'But I really think this is something I should do on my own.' She reached for the door handle and held it ajar.

'I don't mind, dear, honestly. What are mothers for?'

'You and Dad are already doing too much for me,' Claire said tactfully, whilst gently nudging her mother forward. 'If I'm going to live on my own, I should probably take more responsibility.' She felt a lump in her throat as she said the words.

'Oh, okay then,' her mum reluctantly agreed. She looked slightly confused to be out in the hallway. 'If you need me, you know where I am.'

'Thanks.' Claire forced a smile before shutting the door and breathing a sigh of relief. For a moment, she leant against the door, her eyes closed. *Leaving home isn't going to be easy.*

Eventually, she revived her property search. Claire spent a good few hours in the study, in relative solitude; her mother brought in four cups of tea in that time, her eyes scanning the screen furtively as she set each cup down.

Chapter Eighteen

"Remember, another pair of eyes can help as well as hinder"

'You'll never guess who got pulled over by the police the other night.' Beryl's eyes twinkled, and she paused to build tension. 'Only Boozy Bill from number fifty-eight! He finally got caught driving his mobility scooter down Woodlake Road whilst under the influence.'

'I'm glad,' grunted Gladys. 'I've always said he'd be the death of someone in that thing. It's a main road, for crying out loud! Some lunatics go racing down there, without a care for on old man on a scooter. Maybe that'll teach him to keep off the roads, now the police are watching him.'

'I doubt it.' Doreen shook her head adamantly. 'That scooter is the only way he gets home from the pub. Boozy Bill would never dream of giving up his nights out.'

'Boozy Bill wouldn't be Boozy Bill if he didn't go to the pub,' Lissy pointed out.

Rene nodded. 'Exactly.'

Gladys tutted.

The Bitches had gossiped about the locals for almost half an hour. Even Lissy had chipped in occasionally, after recognising some of the names that had been the topics of conversation week in, week out.

Claire hadn't said a word. Her eyes were glued to her needles.

'What's the matter, dear?' Rene said softly, breaking off from the group conversation. 'I haven't heard a peep out of you all afternoon.'

'Oh, nothing really.' Claire stopped knitting for a moment. 'Just thinking about things.'

'Well, you've a lot to think about, what with your job, and moving out.' Rene smiled at her.

Claire pulled a face. 'I can't move out if I can't find somewhere to move to. Home hunting is a nightmare! It doesn't help that Mum is constantly breathing down my neck.'

'I'm sure you'll sort something.' Rene patted Claire's leg. 'Your mother's just trying to help. She's probably more nervous than you are about you leaving. I remember when my Mandy flew the nest. I felt sick for days.'

'But she's not giving me room to breathe, Rene. She's trying to encourage me to move forward and grow, but she's not giving me the space to do it. It's just…frustrating.'

'You could look at houses round at my place,' Adrian offered, suddenly appearing at the table. 'My laptop is at your disposal. And I promise I'll not pass comment on anything you look at. Unless you ask me to, of course.'

'Oh, thank you,' she said. 'But I'll be okay. I'm just having a whinge, as you do.' She turned back to her knitting; out the corner of her eye she saw Adrian shaking his head.

'Honestly, it's no trouble,' he persisted. 'In fact,' Adrian glanced at the table full of potential eavesdroppers and lowered his voice, 'I'd quite like your company.'

Claire met his gaze. She felt the now-familiar charge of electricity shoot through her veins as she did so. *Was it time to stop fighting it?* The floral scent she'd smelt on Adrian in the car the other night didn't seem quite as potent now. 'Well, if you insist…' she heard herself saying. 'That would be great. Thank you.'

Adrian left to serve a customer, grin in place. Claire looked back at the table of knitters. They were all completely silent, and each one had a wide smile on their face.

*

After collecting her and bringing her to his home, Claire could see Adrian had already been busy preparing for her visit. The laptop was charged and powered on, and he'd got all the ingredients ready for a stir-fry, which he started to cook once he'd sat Claire down with a coffee. He wanted them to eat early so that they could get down to business, he said.

I could get used to this. Claire sighed happily and snuggled further into the sofa. She dreamed of coming home every night to Adrian and a plate of piping-hot food. *Mmm…delicious.* She let her imagination drift just a second longer… *Stop it!* She sat up straighter and reprimanded herself. *Tonight is strictly business. A friend doing a friend a favour.* Despite her attempts at self-restraint, an image of a shirtless Adrian, offering her a huge wedge of homemade chocolate fudge cake, popped into her head. *For God's sake, Claire, it's purely platonic..!*

A vibrating noise jolted her from her daydreams. Adrian had left his phone on the coffee table whilst he made their tea, and now someone was trying to reach him. She hesitated for a second - should she ignore it, so that it would go to voicemail, or disturb him in the kitchen? She opted for the latter and reached across; as she caught sight of the screen, however, she saw a name she didn't recognise. *Joanna? Who's Joanna? He's never mentioned a 'Joanna' before.*

Claire changed her mind and left the phone to ring out.

'Dinner is served,' Adrian announced, as he came into the living room. He carried two plates piled high with noodles and veg. 'Bon appetit!'

'Thank you.' Claire battled to dismiss more mental images of a shirtless Adrian, who was now French. She felt heat rise in her cheeks as she took a steaming plate from him. As she tucked into Adrian's delicious stir-fry, all thoughts of Joanna, whoever she was, dissipated.

After they'd eaten, Adrian joined her on the sofa. The search for a suitable property began. 'That one's in a nice area.' Adrian pointed to one of the pictures on the screen, and moved in closer to get a better look. Claire clicked on it. When the details loaded, she let out a sigh. 'It's only one bedroom.'

'Sorry?' Adrian looked at her, confusion on his face. 'I thought you only needed one bedroom? We're looking for a place for you, right?'

'Yes, but what if I have guests? Where will they sleep?' She shook her head. 'No, no. It won't do.' She clicked the 'back' button.

'Um…okay. You're the boss.'

Neither of them said anything for a few minutes. The clicking of the mouse and Claire's fingers on the keyboard provided the only sound. Her eyes were glued to the screen as property after property flew past. Adrian opened his mouth on more than one occasion, but his words never made it to the air.

Whether he wasn't sure if he'd be able to say anything right in Claire's eyes, or the computer's acoustics were simply hypnotic, Adrian stayed silent and gave a huge yawn. He stretched out his arm and curled it around her back in a loose hug.

Claire shifted her eyes from the screen for a moment. She met his gaze and smiled. 'What?' Adrian asked in mock confusion, though his usual grin was in place. She rolled her eyes and laughed. As she turned back, Adrian gave her shoulder a small squeeze and shuffled in closer. *Purely platonic, Claire, remember?* Adrian smelled so good; he smelled like himself again: an intoxicating mix of homemade pastry, fresh linen and his musky cologne.

'That one!' Claire snapped back to the task at hand.

'Huh?'

'I had a friend who lived in that block of flats. It was a nice place, really roomy.' She clicked the image and waited for the page to load. At first glance, the place seemed great. It was a two-bedroom apartment with a spacious kitchen and a generous bathroom. And it was only a five-minute walk from a bus stop whose route went directly to Blossom Hill Surgery. Claire was pretty much sold, then she spotted a flaw. 'It doesn't have a garden,' she said. Her shoulders dropped and she gave a huge sigh.

'A garden?' Adrian gave her a funny look. 'Don't you have hayfever?' Claire nodded, not meeting his eyes. 'And

I thought you hated the whole al-fresco lifestyle.'

She squirmed. 'But it would be nice to have the choice,' she mumbled, quickly scrolling on to the next property.

'Hmm…' Adrian began, but stopped when his phone began to vibrate. He leant forward and, without even looking at who was ringing, rejected the call. As soon as he sat back, the phone went again. At the third attempt, Adrian rolled his eyes and picked up the call. It was a woman on the other end of the line.

'This isn't a good time. Can I call you back?' Adrian's voice carried a hint of panic.

Sat so close to Adrian, Claire could hear the woman's reply: 'Why? Oh, is she there?'

'Yes,' said Adrian. He turned his back a little.

'Oh, sorry. I thought I should let you know that—'

'Hold on.' Adrian gestured to Claire that he was going in the next room. The conversation fell out of earshot.

Left alone, Claire spent a few more minutes idly scrolling through more properties when she came across a picture she recognised. The cursor hovered over the image of 27a St. John's Court. *When had she seen this place before?*

She clicked the link, which brought up the property details. They read: *St. John's Court is situated just thirty minutes from the city centre of Burlington. But although close to the heart of this urban area, it has a rural feel, due to the well-tended communal garden.*

Only thirty minutes away from Burlington? That's it! The bus she'd taken to the Blossom Hill welcome event had driven past it, and she remembered the building catching her eye. She'd thought at the time how nice the flats looked, and how she'd love to have one like that…one day. Claire flicked through the flat images. 27a looked to be an ideal flat for a single lady in her first home. It was spacious, but not too big. It had a fully-kitted kitchen, a bedroom big enough for a king-size bed, a study that could become a second bedroom if needed, and a bathroom with an actual bath. Claire's eyes twinkled.

Flat 27a is situated on the third floor, with easy access from the stairs and the lift. A spacious two-bedroom flat with a fully furnished kitchen, viewing is recommended.

Could this be it? Could this be the one? Claire clicked through the photos again. *There must be something wrong with it.* A loose floorboard. A stone-age alarm system. A 'no pets' restriction policy. She searched and searched, but apartment 27a St. John's Court appeared absolutely perfect. Claire hardly dare breathe - by some miracle she'd found the flat of her dreams.

She didn't know whether to punch the air at the thought of potentially buying the flat of her dreams, or tremble with fear that it would be snapped up before she could make it hers. She started to get up, to ask Adrian what he thought, but remembered he was on the phone.

His call had already taken up forty minutes, during which time, Claire had requested a viewing of 27a St. John's Court via e-mail. For the time being, her property search was complete. She felt excited at what the evening had delivered, and felt there was no point staying to scroll through more properties when the perfect flat had shown itself.

She switched off Adrian's laptop, collected her bag, and retrieved her bus pass from the depths of her purse. She took out a pen and an old receipt and scribbled Adrian a note: *It sounds like you're busy, so I've gone home. Thanks for the use of the laptop, though, I've made good progress! – Claire.*

She finished the note with just her name, no kisses. But she found she couldn't leave without adding a couple. *Damn you, emotions!*

As she headed for Adrian's front door she could tell his conversation was still in full swing. She walked slowly down his garden path, glumly wondering how long it would take before he'd actually realise she'd gone.

Chapter Nineteen

"Every puzzle can have a missing piece"

'Ladies!' Claire couldn't wait to share her news as she walked through the door of Oddballs. 'I have an announcement.'

All eyes were on Claire. Every ear was pricked, awaiting her words. She ached to share her news with someone. There was no time to waste, or she feared she may explode. 'I have a viewing for a flat next week!' The Bitches cheered.

'That's fantastic news, Claire,' said Rene, as she gave the younger woman's hand a squeeze.

'Thank you, Rene.'

'So, you found somewhere then.' Lissy was beaming.

'I did. Finally!' Claire gave a sigh of relief. 'I've just got to hope it lives up to my expectations. From the photographs, Lissy, I know you'd love it.'

'What's it like?' asked Doreen. Claire whipped out her phone and showed the ladies 27a St. John's Court on the estate agent's website.

'Ooh, very swish!' squealed Lissy.

'Very modern and spacious,' agreed Doreen.

'And it's got a well-equipped kitchen. Is that part of the deal?' said Beryl.

'I think so,' said Claire.

'When's your viewing?' said Gladys.

'Next week, at one o'clock,' Claire replied. 'There weren't any other options, apparently. I don't know how long I'll take to look round the flat, and the transport between here and there isn't fantastic…so I'll probably miss our next session. Sorry, ladies.'

'Oh, don't worry about that,' said Gladys. 'Just make sure you call one of us afterwards, to tell us all the details.'

Beryl grabbed her phone from her bag and started waving it around. 'You could TimeFace me.' She beamed. 'Video calling,' she said to Rene knowingly, talking slowly like it was another language. 'It's the future.' Rene just stared at her blankly.

They spent the rest of the afternoon with their heads down, their needles clicking away. Conversation centred on how many housewarming gifts could be knitted, as well as playful bickering over who would create the ideas that had potential. By four o'clock Doreen had finally won the battle to be the one to make Claire a fancy lace table runner.

When the session finished and the group dispersed, Claire wandered towards the till counter, feigning interest in the button display. Adrian was trying to work something out on a piece of paper, a frown on his face. 'Hey, I'm sorry about the other night. I didn't intend being on the phone that long. It was very rude of me.' He fidgeted with his pen.

'It's okay, don't worry about it.' She shrugged off his apology and gave him a smile. 'It turned out well, that's what's important.'

'Oh, yes. I couldn't help overhearing you have a viewing next week.'

'Next Tuesday. I'm gutted I'll miss the Stitch and Bitch, though.'

'Why, what time's your viewing?'

'One o'clock,' she said. 'I won't make it back here by two.'

'Let me take you.'

'Don't be silly. What about the shop?'

'I'll take a later lunch.' He nudged her with his elbow. 'Go on. Let me make it up to you for the other night. Public transport will take ages; I can easily take you and have you back here in time for the session.'

'What about your lunch? I don't want to see you starve!'

'I'll eat my sandwiches in the car. It won't be that different from eating them in the office.' He smiled.

Claire deliberated. A quick, easy journey to the viewing, no panicking about bus times, being able to catch the Stitch and Bitch after all...and time with Adrian. 'Okay, you've twisted my arm. As long as you're sure.'

'Positive. And I'll make sure my phone's turned off too,' he added with a wink.

*

The next week, at eleven fifty-eight, Claire waited at the top of her street wrestling with her thoughts. She'd made the decision to dress smartly, but as she stood in her white shirt, grey skirt and matching grey blazer, she began to dither and worry that she was overdressed. First impressions always count, she reasoned. *But shouldn't the flat be trying to impress me?*

She was still pondering the thought when Adrian arrived. So much so, that for the first part of the journey, Claire didn't pay him much attention. She knew he was wearing his big grey coat, his black skinny jeans, and his beloved scarf of many colours. But the butterflies were starting to churn in her stomach, and it made it difficult to concentrate on anything else. She was on the way to her first ever flat viewing, the first step towards independence.

She tried to think of something else. Rene popped into her head; apparently, she'd called at the shop before Adrian left to pick Claire up, just so she could pass on good luck wishes. She'd said that the other ladies were looking forward to hearing all about it. Rene's kindness made Claire relax a little.

Lost in thought, it took her a moment to register what Adrian had said. 'You look nice,' he repeated. She turned to look at him properly, and that was when she saw it.

Right there, slap bang in the middle of his left cheek, was a large, round fluorescent pink lipstick stain. How he'd managed to get in the car without someone bringing it to his attention, Claire would never know. It was smeared onto his skin, just below his cheekbone. The colour was bright and garish; it was clear Adrian had no idea it was there.

She turned her attention to the road ahead. But however hard she tried, she couldn't stop her eyes wandering back for another look, then another, then another. The lips must have been parted when they kissed him, because there was a flash of skin between the two pink marks. The outline of the kisser's lips were well-preserved, an almost perfect trace of her, whoever she was.

Claire felt anger bubbling in her stomach. She pressed her own lips together so hard they began to go numb. *What could she do?* Adrian was a free man. He had the right to kiss who he wanted, see who he wanted, and do whatever he wanted - with whomever he wanted. But thinking about Adrian with someone else made her heart ache. Their 'relationship' had been a yo-yo affair at the best of times – if there had been a relationship at all. Really, who was Claire to him? A friend? *A fling?*

Even if Claire had grounds for complaint, how could she say so? 'I don't think you should be kissing other people, because we almost kissed, like, three times, and…well…' She'd sound pathetic.

So, as Adrian drove on, the lip-shaped beacon on his face shining brightly, Claire kept quiet. Her body language told its own story, though; her fists were clenched, her face was stony, and her breathing was heavy.

After a few minutes of silence, Adrian glanced at her, and found her sitting like a statue - hard and cold. 'Are you okay?' Claire didn't respond. 'Nerves?' he added. 'They get the best of us sometimes. You'll be fine. At the end of the day, you are the customer. They should be bending over backwards for you, not the other way round.' Claire mustered a curt nod. They were silent for the rest of the journey.

Before long, they pulled into a car park opposite St. John's Court. She'd made it without creating a scene; all she had to do now was calmly step out of the car and cross the road. Simple.

But as Adrian pulled up the handbrake, Claire snapped. 'Is this a joke to you, Adrian? Is this whole thing just some kind of huge, hilarious joke?'

Blindsided, Adrian frowned. 'What?'

'What is that?' Claire flipped the sun visor down so that he could look in the small mirror behind it.

Adrian studied his reflection before wiping away the fuchsia pink stain with his hand. He laughed to himself then turned to face Claire, who clearly did not find it funny. 'Oh, Claire you don't think—'

She cut him off. 'You know what? I don't want to hear any excuses. Us. This, Adrian, whatever it is. It ends here. Today is a new beginning for me, and I've had it with your childish games.'

'Woah. Slow down.' Adrian's eyes were like saucers. 'You make it sound like we're in a relationship or something.'

For a second Claire forgot to breathe. *So, I'm nothing to him?* She shot him an icy glare. 'Regardless, this is not how you treat a lady, girlfriend or not. Goodbye, Adrian.' She got out of the car and slammed the passenger door so hard, she thought the handle might drop off. As she walked away, she heard the other car door slam, and Adrian calling her name.

Claire found the wind refreshing against the heat of her skin. She heard the crunch of footsteps on gravel and guessed that Adrian was trying to catch up with her. She couldn't take it; she didn't want him anywhere near her anymore. She'd given him too many chances. She took the opportunity to sprint across the road and out of sight.

As she approached the entrance to the block of flats she saw a thin woman in a navy suit; she held a clipboard and was glancing from side to side expectantly. Claire kept her head down and strode past her quickly as she heard Adrian's car start. She turned round the next corner, and kept turning until the main road was completely out of sight.

At that point, she stopped and took a deep breath. She could feel adrenaline pumping through her veins. After a few moments she'd calmed down a little.

She reviewed her situation. She was in the back streets of Burlington's outskirts, trying to hide from her ex-man friend, and an estate agent. She had no idea where she was, nor how she was going to get home. Claire slumped down onto a small wall behind her. Of all the ways she'd imagined today would end, this was not one of them.

She noticed a bus stop further up the street, on the other side, and rummaged around in her handbag for her bus pass. She crossed the road and joined the back of the queue for the bus, breathing a sigh of relief. Her eyes wandered down the queue of people standing with her. To her dismay, she realised they were all wearing the same combination of grey trousers and navy blazers, identical crest emblems embroidered on right breast pockets. It was then she tuned in to the giggling and high-pitched squealing around her. She'd just joined the queue for the end-of-lunch-break bus.

Claire searched for someone, anyone, over the age of sixteen, but there was just her and a bunch of kids. She was reminded of all the annoying bus journeys she'd ever taken, cramped up in the corner, her face practically pressed against the window, because it was peak travel time for schoolkids.

She remembered the time a wasp flew in through the bus window and the mad, frantic panic and musical chairs that had ensued, so no one got stung. Or the copious amount of times a bus hadn't shown up, making her late for so many things. Then the night she'd waited in the rain with a soggy Indian takeaway popped into her head, after storming out of Muscles' flat.

She felt like she'd come such a long way since that night. She'd rediscovered the passion for her hobby, made a completely new group of friends - who she genuinely believed loved her like family; and she was heading for a new job, in a new environment. She was also in the process of moving out of her parents' house, to live on her own. She'd even found a new man, until ten minutes ago.

But where was she right now? Stood at a bus stop with a bunch of schoolkids, running away from every dream she'd started chasing.

Claire straightened her skirt, clasped her handbag tightly, then strode off in the direction she'd come. She hadn't come this far to take a step backwards. Not for Adrian, not for anyone.

'Excuse me,' Claire called. The estate agent was tottering on her heels towards a fancy silver car. 'Sorry, I'm Claire. I'm here for a flat viewing. So sorry I'm a little late. Is it still okay to take a look?'

The lady swivelled round, her eyes narrowing as she looked Claire up and down. She huffed but made her way back to the flat. *I'm only fifteen minutes late.* Surely the estate agent lady could forgive her fifteen minutes. The traffic could have been bad. She could have got lost; the estate agent didn't know what could have happened. Claire wasn't about to let her walk away.

'You're very lucky,' the agent sniffed. 'I was about to drive away.' She reached into her handbag and produced a set of keys. The keyring said 27a. 'Come on then, follow me.'

Chapter Twenty

"If you speak, be prepared to listen"

'No, no. Thank you. You've made my day! Yes. Okay then. Thanks again. Speak to you soon. Bye.' Claire ended the call. She'd just finished a manic shift at Dovedon surgery; at the moment, she had paperwork coming out of her ears. Transferring and filing medical records and important documents, both physically and digitally, was her life right now. She hadn't given the flat much thought over the last couple of days, then her phone had started ringing when she was on the bus.

A wide grin spread across her lips. Her application had been accepted. Flat 27a St. John's Court was going to be her new home. Claire practically skipped up her garden path. She bounced through the front door and heard her parents in the kitchen. *The big announcement can wait until dinner.* She raced up the stairs. *But telling Lissy, that can't wait another second!*

'Darling,' her mother called after her. 'A letter came for you today. I've left it on your bedside table.'

'Thanks, Mum.' Claire called back. 'I won't be long.'

She puzzled for a moment. She never got letters. *Who would write to her?* Without warning, Claire's mind conjured up an image of Adrian, and she felt a knot in her stomach. They hadn't spoken since the day of the flat viewing, and Claire was starting to wonder if they ever would. Stitch and Bitch was tomorrow, and she'd been wrestling with herself about whether she should go.

Half of her wanted the mystery letter writer to be Adrian, but the other half of her would be happy if she never saw or heard from him again. She plucked the envelope from her night stand and instantly recognised Adrian's lanky scrawl. She quickly tore open the envelope; inside was a small piece of card. It read: *I've booked a taxi for you at 7pm. I can explain everything. Love A. x*

She stared at the note. *Adrian had booked a taxi for…where? Why was he bothering? And most importantly…why had he written 'love'?*

Should she go? If she went, all efforts to erase Adrian from her mind would likely be made more difficult. On the other hand, he looked to be offering answers that she knew, deep down, she wanted to hear. Her mind was already made up. And even if it had wavered, her heart would have made her go.

She now had another decision to make. What should she wear? *This old chestnut again.* She sighed and turned to her wardrobe. She soon realised this was much harder than when she'd agonised over her outfit for the Blossom Hill event.

She wasn't going to impress anyone, she concluded finally, she was going to listen. Immediately, that ruled out her pretty frocks and floaty blouses, and she didn't even look at the rainbow of knitted garments taking up most of the wardrobe space. Eventually, she chose a mint green jumper dress - shop bought - and a pair of stretchy leggings for comfort.

She dressed, then went to put on her black leather boots. She needed socks first, which was often a problem; she had a habit of losing socks, or she managed to put holes in them with very little effort.

With none in her drawer, she glanced at the washing pile her mother had left at the foot of her bed that morning. Without any need for searching, she spotted a pair of bright pink socks sat smugly on the top. She snatched them up and pulled them onto her feet. 'You haven't won yet, Adrian,' she muttered.

The taxi arrived promptly at seven o'clock. Claire sat in the back and initially exchanged small talk with the driver before spending the rest of journey with her eyes on the road, looking for any clue towards their destination. It had turned dark now, and it was raining. The water danced down the taxi windows, distorting the light from street lamps and headlights, merging them together in swirls and explosions.

Claire began to recognise her surroundings and relaxed. Minutes later, the taxi pulled up outside a familiar bungalow with leaded windows. She spotted small puffs of smoke coming from the brick chimney and smiled, despite herself. Adrian was outside already, under a large, black umbrella. She watched as he paid the taxi driver and came to open her door.

'I'm so glad you came,' he said. She could hear the relief in his voice. He offered his hand and helped her out of the taxi. 'Let's get inside, out of the cold and rain.'

Once in the hall, Adrian took Claire's coat. *Such chivalry!* She suddenly realised that it wasn't that unusual, but something Adrian routinely practised.

She bent down to unzip her boots. As she handed them to him, she caught him looking at her socks, a smile on his face. 'They were the only ones I could find…' she said, as firmly as she could, not wanting him to read anything into it. But her voice came out squeaky rather than dismissive; just being back in his company had caused her bravado to melt. Though she'd physically softened, her mind didn't let her forget what had happened between them. *How can it ever be okay?*

'Oh, right.' Adrian's smile dropped. He gestured through to the living room. 'Go through. I just need to check on some things then I'll be right with you.'

Claire felt that the atmosphere was tense and way too formal. She scurried into the living room. As she reached the doorway she stopped, touched by the sight before her. Adrian's home always had a cosy, cluttered feel to it, a characteristic left behind by his mother, and aptly demonstrated by the faux flower arrangements and pastel dollies dotted about everywhere.

This evening, all objects, ornaments and pieces of furniture were lined up against the walls. Stood alone, in the centre of the room, was a table and two chairs. Adrian had laid the table so that it was both minimalistic and romantic: a plain white tablecloth, silverware, and two tall white candles in the centre. They flickered away in the dim light. The atmosphere immediately switched to sensual and welcoming. It was more intimate than any setting Claire had experienced, including the fancy restaurant Adrian had taken them to on their date night, which seemed like light years ago.

Adrian came up behind her, making her jump. He placed a calming hand on her shoulder. 'Please, take a seat. I hope you haven't eaten. I'm cooking for us.'

He brought out two wine glasses and a bottle from behind his back. He poured them both a glass as Claire pulled back a chair. He then took the seat opposite.

She had his full attention and she shuffled awkwardly under his gaze. 'No, I haven't,' she said.

She suddenly remembered the big announcement she'd planned to deliver to her parents over dinner.

'Good.'

An awkward silence followed. Claire allowed herself to look at him for the first time since she'd arrived. She knew it would be painful, which is why she'd restrained herself.

He wore his tight black jeans, and a purple and navy checked shirt. His fringe was swept to the side, out of his eyes. His gaze was intense, and concern was etched on his face, behind his black frames.

She panicked and broke eye contact. As her gaze lowered, she noticed his hand-knitted burgundy bow-tie. Without thinking, she leaned over and straightened it.

'Thanks.' Adrian let out a small chuckle.

'You're welcome,' she said, sitting back in her seat.

She heard him take a deep breath. 'If I thought you'd have answered my calls, texts, emails, or voicemails, I would have sorted everything out between us a lot sooner. It's got so out of hand. I'm sorry.' He paused. 'So…I decided that the only way to do this was face to face. No more miscommunications. All questions answered. No more mystery.'

Perhaps sensing that Claire wasn't about to speak, he continued, 'When I got back to the car last Tuesday I was so angry. It's so silly. Really, it is. But I never had the chance to explain before you ran off. Why didn't you mention it sooner?'

Claire shrugged. She wasn't going to let Adrian pass the blame onto her, but she kept quiet.

'I'm surprised that, when you calmed down, you didn't realise yourself where it had come from. I only know one lady who wears such an outrageous shade of pink.' Adrian gave Claire a moment to come up with the answer, but she wasn't in the mood for guessing games and shrugged again.

'Rene kissed my cheek when she popped in to say "good luck"; she knew how excited you were about the flat. I had no idea she'd marked me until you mentioned it.'

Claire blushed. Now she thought about it, she recognised the shade as Rene's trademark pink 'hot lips', as she called them. That it had missed Adrian's cheekbone made even more sense; Rene was a lot shorter than Claire. But even if that was the case, the lipstick had only been one issue. Rene wasn't to blame for the rest of them.

Adrian obviously had a girlfriend, but he'd made Claire feel that he wanted to be with her at the same time. Maybe he had more than one lady friend. Abi. Joanna. *Who else?*

'The lipstick was just the last straw, Adrian. Rene doesn't wear awful perfume that smells like rotting flowers, nor is she called Abi. And she doesn't own a mobile phone and call you for long chats when you've got company, unlike Joanna.

Adrian eyes widened. He opened his mouth to talk but stopped and shook his head. 'I'm not quite sure I'm following,' he said eventually. 'I didn't realise there was so much to this.' He looked perplexed. 'Let's take them one at a time,' he added softly. 'I'm sure I can explain them all. I want to get this right.'

'Your coat. When you picked me up after Doctor Samuel's welcome party…it smelt like a florist's at the end of the season!' Claire's voice became strained.

'Ah, the welcome party. What day was that?"

'Friday.'

'That one's easy. I have a regular, Mrs Brown, on Fridays. Wonderful lady, but she likes her floral perfumes very strong. I know her scent followed me around that day, because it stuck up my nose, but I didn't realise it had stuck to my clothes.' *Well, yes, that could have happened. But that still didn't explain everything.*

'Okay, let's leave that one. Who's Joanna?' Adrian let out a deep sigh. *This is it, he does have someone…*

He twiddled with his cutlery. 'I wanted it to be a surprise. This is not how I imagined telling you. But now you've asked…'

Claire braced herself for the news he was in a relationship. And that he was deliriously happy.

'Joanna is a friend who's done me a favour. Her mum and my mum were really good friends. We grew up together, and by proxy, we both caught the knitting bug. She lives down south now, so I don't get to see her very often, but we talk and text a lot.'

Claire nodded, not sure where this was going.

'She's been trying to organise a retreat for all her knitting friends - a scenic holiday, where everyone lives together for a week and, well, knits. She took her mum as a surprise last year and they loved it. I asked if she could book me two places. I thought it might help you with your knitting issues…and a bit of sea air never hurt anyone! She phoned to say that the cottage she'd reserved had double-booked our week. We were trying to match our diaries so we could reschedule.' He smiled. His eyes glittered in the candlelight.

Claire felt awful. All this time she'd thought he was stringing her along with other women, and he'd instead been planning a trip away for them both. Now she knew, she couldn't help but feel ashamed at how silly she'd been. Adrian had only ever shown her kindness, and all she'd offered was bitterness. She'd been blind to his intentions; she'd jumped to conclusions, and invented misunderstandings without even giving him the opportunity to explain. She'd acted like a bitch, and still Adrian was here, trying.

She felt herself welling up; she couldn't believe she'd been so stupid. She could feel her defences melting away, but there was one last point she needed answering.

'And Abi?' She watched as Adrian ran his fingers through his fringe in exasperation.

'We've been through this.' He looked at her with pleading eyes. 'Abi is just a friend.' He paused, then added, 'But if it bothers you that much, I will never speak to her again. Claire, you mean so much to me, and if the last seven days have taught me anything, it's that I need you in my life. So, if that's what it takes…okay.'

She didn't know what to say. She suddenly became aware of her heart thudding rapidly in her chest, and knew that the tears in her eyes threatened to fall. *Was he saying what she thought he was saying?* She could see he was vulnerable, aware that he'd left himself wide open. He shifted awkwardly, clearly out of his comfort zone. What he'd said wasn't borne of excuses or lies; it was the truth. He'd put his heart on the line.

Deep down inside, she knew that all her previous thoughts were wrong. It was her turn to be honest. She looked into his eyes and smiled. 'I'm sorry for doubting you.' There was a brief moment in which the pair just looked at one another, tears glistening in their eyes.

'So…' Adrian prompted, tentatively.

'I believe you,' she said, a smile curling at the edges of her lips. 'I'm just sorry that it came to this...I'm sorry for all the confusion. I want to put things right.' She got up from her seat and moved around the table. 'I've been meaning to do something for a while. Had it not been for all the misunderstandings, it would've happened by now.' Intuitively, Adrian pushed his chair back as Claire approached, and she sat, snugly, in his lap.

The pair were nose to nose, where they'd been many times before; but this was not going to be another near miss, Claire vowed. She leaned in, and slightly tilted her head, happy to see that Adrian was mirroring her.

Their lips finally met.

Claire melted. Adrian's lips were soft and full, and he tasted delicious. Their kiss was slow but meaningful. It lingered, with neither wanting to break away. When they finally pulled apart, they gazed into each other's eyes. She let out a small sigh. *Finally.*

Adrian coughed awkwardly and his cheeks coloured. 'I, um, better check on the food.'

Adorable... She made no effort to move. 'Before you go, I've got some news.'

'Yeah?'

'You know Flat number 27a?' Adrian nodded. 'Well, it will soon be mine!'

'That's fantastic!' He gave her an affectionate squeeze.

'I know, right?' She hooked her fingers into the front of Adrian's shirt. 'How about another one of those kisses to celebrate?' She pulled him in close and their lips met again.

She eventually jumped off his lap so that he could see to the food. The aromas wafting in from the kitchen smelled absolutely amazing. But however keen she was to eat the sumptuous dinner Adrian had prepared, she knew that he'd prove more delicious.

Chapter Twenty-One

"The end of one chapter is also the beginning of the next"

Claire looked down at the tiny bundle she was cradling. The baby looked so snug, wrapped up in her hand-knitted blanket - her tiny fists clenched tightly around it. *I could spend all day cuddling this little one...* The Bitches stood around them, all smiling and cooing at the little bundle, too. *Oh, Alice Irene Richards, you little heartbreaker!*

'She's beautiful, Jess. Congratulations.' Claire didn't want to let go, but little Alice began to whimper and fidget. 'I think she wants Mummy.'

'Thanks.' Jess positively glowed as she took Alice back into her embrace. Rene was glowing too; she was full of smiles and had rosy-red cheeks. It was one of those moments that belonged in a photo frame. Picture perfect.

'It'll be your turn next,' Rene said to Claire, though she winked at Adrian.

'Oh,' Claire felt herself blushing, 'maybe not just yet.' As she turned to look at Adrian she saw him smile and wink back at Rene.

'Don't you worry, Adie, if the time comes and you can't stomach it, you know where I am. I'm a fully qualified birthing partner now, you know!' Everyone laughed.

'I'll bear it in mind.' He chuckled and snaked his arm across Claire's shoulders. 'Thank you for bringing Alice to visit, it was very sweet of you.'

Jess put the baby back in her pram and tucked her in. 'No problem.'

The wait to meet little Alice in the flesh seemed to have taken forever. Since moving out, Claire felt like time had slowed down. She wasn't complaining; she was making the most of it.

'We wanted to come and see you, didn't we, Jess? I'll be back here with you girls soon.' Rene gestured to the empty seat at the table.

'Go! Enjoy it,' said Gladys. 'They don't stay tiny for long.' She lifted up her knitting. With the school holidays almost upon them, she was knitting at double her usual speed, to make sure all her family's new-term jumpers would be ready in time.

Rene laughed. 'Best of luck with that, Gladys. Take care, all, and enjoy that holiday of yours, you two!' There came a noisy few minutes, as everyone said their goodbyes. Then the bell above the shop door rang and they were gone.

'I keep forgetting you're going away. When do you go again?' asked Beryl.

'Tomorrow.' Claire grinned. Joanna and Adrian had managed to find a suitable date, so the knitting retreat was on. For months, she'd tried to contain her excitement; she couldn't believe the day was almost upon them.

'I bet you're excited. I'm so jealous,' said Doreen.

'So am I,' Lissy piped up. It was wonderful having a keen knitter as a best friend, Claire decided. Lissy had offered to look after Oddballs whilst Claire and Adrian were away, with help from Doreen. She'd taken some holiday from work, and was really looking forward to it. Her competence and confidence had grown quite quickly; Lissy's shawls were even starting to rival Doreen's. Their passion and skills - Doreen's love of traditional and vintage, and Lissy's devotion to fashion and technology – had seen them open a webstore called 'Vintage Lace'. Together, they created unique, handknitted vintage wear, and they were doing exceptionally well. Lissy had been unable to control her excitement at the Stitch and Bitch session the previous week, because 'Vintage Lace' had topped one thousand 'likes'.

Adrian went to serve a customer and the Bitches fell into an easy silence as their needles clicked away. 'Oh my gosh, with all the excitement I almost forgot!' Beryl suddenly began rooting around in her trolley; after a moment or two she emerged, brandishing an envelope. 'Look what came in the post this morning!'

Inside was a letter and a photograph. Beryl passed the photo around the group. When it reached Claire, she couldn't help but smile. The picture showed a chicken, stood proudly, sporting a fetching knitted jacket in fluorescent green.

Beryl cleared her throat and read the letter to the group: *Dear Beryl. Thank you kindly for your donation of knitted chicken jackets. As a token of our appreciation, we have included a photo of our newest ex-battery hen. We have named her Beryl and, as you can see, she's a very big fan of your work.*

'They say I'm welcome to visit her any time I like.' Beryl's smile was wide.

'Aw, that's fantastic!' said Doreen, passing the photograph back. 'I feel another day trip coming on, don't you, ladies?' There was a chorus of agreement. Instantly, Beryl set about researching transport on her phone.

Just moments later, Gladys put down her needles. 'Right then, until next time, girls.' The other Bitches began to gather up their belongings, too. After saying their goodbyes everyone headed for the door.

'Make sure you take lots of pictures at this retreat. And tell the ladies there about Vintage Lace!' said Lissy.

Claire gave an exaggerated sigh before pulling her into hug. 'I will. Just try not to become too famous whilst I'm away, alright? And any problems—'

Lissy cut her off. 'We'll be fine, honestly. Go enjoy yourselves!'

The bell over the door chimed as the Bitches left. Claire sat back down at the table. Her latest creative project was part of a mystery knit-a-long; she was in the middle of creating a wonderfully intricate throw. The only problem was, she didn't know which colour wools she'd need, something she wouldn't find out until she was knitting with the other participants – apparently, this was the whole point of a mystery knit-a-long. This meant numerous balls of wool were discarded on the knitting table every Tuesday afternoon.

She scooped them all up and stuffed them into her rather large knitting bag. She couldn't wait to finish the throw and spread it across her sofa in her newly-decorated lounge. Six months on, and the flat truly felt like home.

Adrian came over to give her a hand. 'Thanks,' she said, taking the last of the escapee balls from him and packing them away.

'No problem.' He placed the lightest of kisses on her lips. 'You staying until close tonight?'

Claire shook her head. 'No, not tonight. I've got to get the flat ready for later.'

He nodded. 'Oh, yes. Are you absolutely sure you don't need me over any earlier? Even the greatest of cooks have a sous chef.'

'Absolutely sure,' she said confidently. 'I've got this.' And she had. Ever since Claire had learned about the '30-minute meal' cookbook series – after receiving one from Lissy as a house warming gift - her culinary nightmares were a thing of the past. 'You're my guest tonight, too. I want you to enjoy it.' She kissed him back. 'Now, don't let me stop you getting your work done. See you tonight.'

*

Claire walked through the door of 27a and immediately sunk her feet into her cosy slippers waiting by the door. She took off her coat, hung it on the peg, and picked up her post. After pressing the 'play' button on her answering machine, she went into the kitchen and switched the kettle on.

'You have no new messages.'

She sighed contently and popped all the important post into her letter holder. She wasn't letting life just happen to her anymore; she was in control, and she liked the feeling. Her job at Blossom Hill had proved a good decision. She was now one of the surgery's three receptionists. Doctor Samuel's office was on the other side of the surgery to reception, which meant she hardly saw him. Holidays or shift

changes were never a problem, and her fellow receptionists were two of the loveliest people she'd ever met.

With a good couple of hours before her dinner guests
arrived, Claire ran a relaxing, piping hot bath.

*

'This is delicious.' Claire's mum licked her lips and
scooped up another forkful of chicken and mushroom
risotto. Her approval was echoed around the table with
similar murmurs of appreciation.

'Thanks.' Claire beamed. *Another 30-minute success!*

'And I love what you're doing with the place. What do
you call it again? Shaggy chic?'

'*Shabby* chic, Mum.' Claire tried hard not to choke on her
rice. She caught Adrian trying to stifle a laugh, too.

'Oh, that's it, yes. I know we see it every fortnight, but
it's lovely to see the transformation, from flat into home.
Isn't it, George?'

'Mm-mm,' he agreed, his mouth full. He swallowed
and started to cough, which resulted in his wife slapping
his back. 'Lovely,' he said, when he eventually found his
voice.

When the four of them had cleared their plates, they sat
in the living room with coffee and after dinner mints, discussing Adrian and Claire's getaway.

'I'd take at least two breaks during your drive tomorrow,
Adrian. I've heard the service station at Hackway is very
pleasant,' George offered.

Adrian nodded. 'Claire does love her coffee stops.' He
winked at her. She pretended to be offended before breaking into a smile.

'Call us if there are any problems, though I'm sure there
won't be. I just wanted you both to know that you can.'
Her mum twiddled with the hem of her skirt nervously.

'Thanks, Mum.' When Claire first went on holiday with
Muscles, her mother tried to pack their suitcases, and she
insisted Claire's dad drove them there. She even offered to

stay at the hotel across the street for the entire week. *Thank God…she's finally letting go of those reins.*

'So, you've told us many times that this holiday isn't a holiday, but a 'knitting retreat'. What will you be knitting when you're there?' Now that Claire's knitting had come on leaps and bounds, her mum had taken quite an interest.

'Well, I'm doing this throw pattern from the internet. Only, I haven't got all the pattern just yet, because it's a mystery knit-along…' Claire began.

'Another coffee, George?' Adrian took their mugs and headed into the kitchen.

'Oh, yes. Yes please,' he replied. After just a few seconds of the intense discussion between his wife and daughter, concerning the progress of Claire's knitting, he called out, 'Let me give you a hand, son.'

Before long, it was ten o'clock, and Claire's parents were making their way to the door. Her first dinner party had been a success. She felt like jumping for joy. *This 'adult' lark isn't that hard.*

Before she left, her mum pulled her close. 'Your father and I are so happy for you, darling. Make sure you enjoy next week - you've earned it,' she whispered. Claire felt herself welling up. Not knowing what to say, she gave her mum a cuddle, hoping that if she squeezed her tightly enough, she could communicate all the things she couldn't vocalise.

Claire and Adrian watched her parents take the stairs. The pair descended, holding hands, both laughing at something George said. Claire wasn't sure if she'd ever felt so happy. She beamed at Adrian.

'You did it, baby,' he whispered, before bending slightly and kissing her softly on the lips.

An hour later, they climbed into bed. Adrian wriggled towards the centre so he was spooning Claire. He placed his arm over hers and drew her in even closer. 'I'm really proud of you, you know…how you handled tonight and everything.'

'Why, thank you.' Claire snuggled into Adrian's embrace. He placed a few light kisses on her neck. 'Mmm…' she sighed.

'All ready for tomorrow?'

'I think so,' she said. 'You?'

'I can't wait.' He yawned. 'But I think we better get some sleep. We've such an early start in the morning.'

She pouted, but didn't argue. Adrian *was* driving them almost to the other end of the country. 'Okay… I'll get the light.' But instead of reaching for the switch for the lamp, she rolled over and gave Adrian a passionate kiss. His arms wrapped around her more tightly. Eventually, they broke apart.

'Sleep tight, Claire-bear.'

'Sweet dreams, Oddball.'

This time, she reached for the switch. Before she did so, she couldn't help taking one last look at their suitcases, stood side by side near the doorway.

She doubted she'd get any sleep – she was far too excited. She took a moment to think about how far they'd both come, since first crossing paths in Blurb. That day, she'd been looking for 'self-help', and it looked like she'd found it. Because once she'd started to take control of certain aspects in her life, the rest had just fallen into place.

Whatever the adventure sitting on the horizon, Claire wouldn't have to see it through alone. She had all the support she could ever want or need, now Adrian was by her side.

THE END

Acknowledgements

My journey with Claire and Adrian, from head to page, has been long (but very rewarding). Although, at times, writing can be a solitary sport, there are many who have been instrumental in making this book possible. I want to take this opportunity to thank them for their time, encouragement, and ongoing support.

Firstly, to Diane - my editor, agent, publisher and writing guru, all rolled into one! Without you, my dream would never have come true. Thank you for your advice, your honesty, and your guidance. I'd have been lost in this maze without you.

To my friends (yes, Kris, this means you!), thank you for being my cheerleaders. The support network that I have around me is phenomenal. A special thank you to Sandie; without you, this certainly never would have happened.

To my mom: without your love of knitting and books, Unravelled would never have existed. To both my mom and dad, thank you for always believing in me. Your pride can outshine any darkness; never once have you made me feel like my dreams are out of reach. I cannot thank you enough.

To Daisy, the perfect writing buddy. Although you couldn't make it to the finish line, thank you for being with me during the race. Your cuddles were always on cue and you were the first to hear how the story ended.

To the real Rene: sorry about the swearing! But as my nan, I'm sure you're proud.

To Liam, my very own Adrian. Thank you for the endless conversations, the pep talks, the late nights, the early mornings, your ears (which I must have worn out by now!), and your loving heart. Thank you for holding my hand through it all. ♥

And finally - thank you to you, the person holding my book in your hands. Thank you for sharing this amazing journey with me. Honestly, it means the world. And, if you have the time to leave me a review - which will ultimately help more readers discover Claire and Adrian's story for themselves - I would be eternally grateful.

Briony Marshall